Hebdomeros

David Zwirner Books

ekphrasis

Hebdomeros
A novel by Giorgio de Chirico

Introduction by Fabio Benzi

Giorgio de Chirico, *Il ritorno di Ulisse*, 1973. Oil on canvas, 23 ⅝ × 28 ¾ inches | 60 × 73 cm

Introduction

Fabio Benzi

When Giorgio de Chirico published *Hebdomeros*, in French, in 1929, it came as a bolt from the blue in the complex and complicated world of the Parisian avant-garde.

In some ways, it constituted the main act of a muffled war that André Breton and the surrealists at large had undertaken against him, the lethal weapon that de Chirico detonated without advance warning, routing his foes decisively and leaving them without any chance at retaliation.[1]

We should briefly lay the groundwork here. For fairly unseemly and basically financial considerations, Breton undertook a ferocious offensive against the painter in 1926, leveling charges that he had been an intellectual corpse since 1917; this after praising him, in 1924 and 1925, as the pioneer of surrealism.[2] De Chirico had blazed the way to an acceptance of dreams and the subconscious in modern art; he stood as a major landmark in the intellectual constellation that had wheeled overhead at the birth of Breton's movement. But as was later the case for other great artists, the demands and overbearing comportment of surrealism's leader shattered that relationship. Breton used this tactic with others, condemning his old friends as "cadavers" who had simply outlived themselves (for instance, with Raymond Queneau, Georges Bataille, Antonin Artaud, Robert Desnos, Philippe Soupault): de Chirico merely happened to be the first, and surely the greatest, among them.

In the 1920s, surrealism was just one of many avant-garde movements active in Paris; it had not yet attained the central position it would hold after World War II, in part due to the movement's importance to the development of American abstract expressionism. Still, Breton's hostility in no way undercut the fundamental role that de Chirico enjoyed in French and European painting of the 1920s, nor did it alter the esteem he commanded among both critics of the period and many of his fellow artists, including Marcel Duchamp, Max Ernst, and René Magritte. De Chirico—who had been living in Paris since 1925, after spending ten years in Italy following the outbreak of World War I—was in fact one of the most sought-after and renowned painters in Paris at the time, so much so that Jean Cocteau (and he was not alone in this) considered him, together with Picasso (with whom he was close friends), one of the two Dioskouroi (literally, sons of Zeus) among the Parisian avant-garde. Indeed, Breton's visceral hatreds were taken by many of his comrades for exactly what they were: fevered manifestations of abject resentments. Let us look at Duchamp, who was just one of many who sharply denounced Breton's excesses. In 1967, in response to an interviewer's prompt, "You defended de Chirico against the anathema issued by Breton and his friends," Duchamp stated in no uncertain terms: "To come back to Breton: the way they all denounced de Chirico after 1919 was so contrived that it deeply irritated me."[3]

Hebdomeros, an autobiographical novel and de Chirico's masterpiece, comprises utterly unique imagery and reasoning that is anchored in his painting, both ear-

lier and that made contemporaneously with the novel—
it is a work of striking originality and searing lyricism.
Thus, de Chirico bestrode the scene as the unequaled
master of surrealism, which was his own personal creation (the headwater of "one of those stories, so perfectly logical in appearance and so greatly metaphysical
at heart, of which he held the secret and the monopoly," as the artist writes in his novel), at that point being
plundered by the younger surrealists. After all, the man-
uscripts containing his metaphysical texts from 1911 to
1915, at the time in the hands of Jean Paulhan and Paul
Éluard, had been passionately read by the surrealists and
already prefigured, with full maturity, the associative
and visionary surrealist technique.

In fact, even Breton was nonplussed. He tried to
spread a rumor that de Chirico had written the novel
before World War I. (Otherwise, how could an intellectually dead artist, an inert and hollow corpse, have
penned such an impassioned and unquestionably grip-
ping book?) The novel's themes, however, are inextrica-
bly intertwined with more recent aspects of de Chirico's
imaginative world, while the writing style, fast-paced
and stream-of-consciousness inspired, *à bout de souf-
fle* (breathless), undoubtedly dates it to 1928 to 1929.[4]
Breton's baseless doubts failed to take root. The book
was published by Pierre Gaspard Lévy's Éditions du
Carrefour, the publisher of the surrealist journal *Bifur*
(which Lévy edited with Georges Ribemont-Dessaignes,
and which lent its name to the imprint that issued

Hebdomeros) and major books by such surrealist masters as Max Ernst (*La femme 100 têtes*, in 1929, perhaps the most beautiful surrealist illustrated volume). So the bomb basically went off right in the surrealists' home. And, indeed, the surrealists were enchanted by *Hebdomeros*, finding it "an interminably beautiful work."[5] So Breton was left (immediately after the publication of his paradigmatic autobiographical novel *Nadja* in 1928), as they say, *bouche bée*, jaw dropped. De Chirico sent him a dedicated copy (with only two words inscribed on the title page: *très cordialement*). That battle was won.

While the war itself ground on for years (especially after 1945), we are uninterested in its aftermath, for now. Let us limit ourselves to the recollection of this story: in February 1943, during a soiree at Peggy Guggenheim's New York home, Breton, a bit tipsy from too many cocktails, confessed to James Thrall Soby, with reference to *Hebdomeros*, that de Chirico wrote "in French, like an angel, with extraordinary nuances of meaning and thought."[6] *In vino veritas*.

Instead, let's look at the reception that de Chirico's masterpiece met with in Paris. The surrealist magazines (*La Révolution surréaliste*, whose final issue coincided with the publication of *Hebdomeros*, and *Le Surréalisme au service de la révolution*) maintained an ostentatious silence, as was to be expected regarding the ostracism by Breton. Nevertheless, there were several major reviews, quite a few considering that this was an avant-garde work, not just a book of narrative fiction. Indeed, some were authored by big names in French literary and visual culture, mostly on the political left (which implicitly aligned with the artist's ideas, as he openly opposed fascism, as evidenced by a notorious 1927 interview he gave in the magazine *Comoedia*,[7] thereby closing the door to any public exhibitions of his work in Italy for many years).

Hebdomeros was excerpted in advance by the magazine *Bifur* in July 1929, and the book itself must have appeared in bookstores in early 1930. The publication date listed at the end of the book, December 31, 1929, in fact, is rather symbolic as the very last day of the year and remains perfectly in line with the text's supreme ambiguity. The first mention of the novel we find in newspapers dates to November 10, 1929, in a brief notice by the critic René Lalou in *La Quinzaine critique des livres et des revues* that refers to the excerpt in *Bifur*. (Lalou later published another review of the book in the same journal.) On February 1, 1930, the important magazine *Les Nouvelles littéraires* ran an advertisement from the publisher stating: "The most original of painters has written *Hebdomeros*."

The first full review, by the critic and writer Edmond Jaloux, a scholar of Rilke, appeared in *Les Nouvelles littéraires* on February 8, 1930. A great admirer of de Chirico as a painter, Jaloux called out the book's extraordinary and captivating originality, astutely identifying some of its literary references: "a vague echo" of Lautréamont's *Les Chants de Maldoror*, "the solemn style" of certain Poe stories, a hint of Piranesi, Edward Young's

Night Thoughts, and Rimbaud. The review was enthusiastic, praising the novel's hallucinatory framework, the strangeness of the details, the metaphysical disquiet, and the unusual cinematic structure that intersected with archaic Greece and monumental Rome, as well as the unsettling and fascinating series of dreams that cast a veil of tragic gravitas over ghosts, statues, and characters. On February 11, *Comoedia* published a more generic account by Gonzague Truc, a novelist and scholastic philosopher who rightly identified the double of the author in the character of Hebdomeros, "a famous painter [who] believes that his paintings should be 'read' and his literature 'viewed,'" who "wrote about nothing other than what one sees with one's eyes shut."

A brief announcement in the *Paris-Midi* on Saturday, March 8, 1930, reminded readers that de Chirico would be signing copies of *Hebdomeros* that day, from 4 to 7 p.m., at the Galerie Jacques Bonjean, along with recent monographs on his work (in fact, three monographs were published on de Chirico in 1928 alone, written by Jean Cocteau, Waldemar George, and Boris Ternovets; and in 1927, one by Roger Vitrac). A journalistic account appeared in that same newspaper on March 10, informing readers that the gallery, on rue La Boétie, had organized an exhibition of recent works, including a series of self-portraits, by "the great master who, with his sense of mystery, has exerted great influence over an entire contemporary school of art." Many painters and admirers attended, among them the socialites the Count of Saint-Aulaire and the Princesses Paleologue and Ghika, and a mysterious Scandinavian woman (who we suspect may have been de Chirico's lover at the time, the striking Romanian Cornelia Silbermann: we'll find her first name in the book). The reviewer, identified as G. O., also offered a portrait of the artist: "Tall, imposing, with a sharply defined face, topped by a broad forehead, hair fairly long and slightly wavy, utterly calm, serene, except for the deeply marked triple furrow between his brows indicating painful reflection. De Chirico wandered through the gallery, sitting at the signing table only when absolutely necessary; it almost seemed that he wanted to hide."

On March 8, in *Les Nouvelles littéraires*, Jean Cassou, the writer, art scholar, and founder of the Musée National d'Art Moderne in Paris, wrote: "*Hebdomeros*, by the great painter de Chirico, about which Edmond Jaloux recently wrote here, comprises a series of disconcerting and magnificent images, irrefutable sisters to the artist's paintings, immobile visions, at once surprising and grandiose, dreams of an antiquity not unlike that which materialized before the eyes of Thomas De Quincey, the opium eater, when he heard the words *consul romanus*." Cassou displays a thorough familiarity with de Chirico's paintings, and perhaps also his writings, as he seems to allude to something de Chirico wrote in 1920, about Max Klinger, in which he mentions the same dream episode from De Quincey's *Confessions of an English Opium-Eater*.[8] The following day, an article by Nino Frank appeared in *L'Intransigeant*. Frank was an antifascist, a friend of Joyce and his translator into French, and the managing editor of *Bifur*—a remarkable figure in the French and international cultural scene. In his review, Frank admired de Chirico, deemed the "legends" about him planted by the surrealists absurd, and discussed the novel's autobiographical value and its reconciliation between the Mediterranean and the North (comparing the Parthenon with Böcklin's *Isle of the Dead*), clearly recalling the artist's early writings but noting a new "unexpected mood" that "makes his paintings and *Hebdomeros* so poetic and original." Frank also perceptively noted that "Italians don't care much for mystery": a fact that would explain the novel's lack of critical attention in Italy, even when it was finally translated into Italian, under the title *Ebdòmero*, in 1942.

On March 10, the brief but intense second review by Lalou appeared in *La Quinzaine critique des livres et des revues*, where he astutely mentioned Gérard de Nerval as one of de Chirico's sources, in addition to Poe and Lautréamont. Lalou identified "the atmosphere of irresistible lyrical flow," produced "by the long sinuous descriptions in which Hebdomeros's monologues blossom," without "any division into chapters across 253 pages," as the surrealistic structure that undergirds the book's meaning. *La Revue belge*, on April 1, 1930, featured an editorial that read: "Then, from these pages, one feels the vast breath, the fertile warmth of Mother-Poetry, progenitrix of the gods. *Hebdomeros* is the most accurate Atlas of the Currents of Mystery yet composed, at the service of the greatest navigators, as well as those rare explorers possessed by a 'different' sort of curiosity."

Michel Leiris, in the magazine *Documents*, edited by the former surrealist Georges Bataille, spoke of the book (in issue 5, June 1930, in which he dates the publication to 1930, suggesting it must have appeared around the turn of the year) in grandiose terms and simultaneously with an awkward discomfort: "A noble but interminable stroll, to the agony of gladiators obliged to remain frozen at attention before you … de Chirico's *Hebdomeros* (all kidding aside) radiates absolute greatness, but greatness itself can be annoying, as annoying as the god Terminus or any form of genius that, without pausing before the continuous stream of miracles, lets fall an eternal rain." In the April 15, 1931, edition of *Europe*, the journal founded by Romain Rolland, Paul Nizan reviewed the book, expressing his appreciation ("de Chirico is a great painter, now he seems to be every bit as much a poet") but establishing a certain distance from the magic that inevitably leads to celestial greatness: the novel was too far from practical human problems which Nizan personally felt were of greater contemporary urgency.

If the renown of the novel continued uninterrupted in the realm of literary criticism in France—though in a largely generic fashion, taken as a masterpiece of surrealist literature—it vanished in Italy, without much of a trace, upon its publication there in 1942. After all, as Nino Frank had observed, "Italians don't care much for mystery." De Chirico had offered the book to Giovanni Scheiwiller and at least one other publisher as early as 1928. But Scheiwiller was not publishing literary works at that time. Another attempt at publication took place in 1938, undertaken by Libero de Libero for Edizioni della Cometa: for unknown, maybe economical, reasons, it failed, too. When the book finally appeared, in 1942, the cover emphasized: "This is a famous book unknown to Italians. Written in Italian, translated by the author into French." The issue of the novel's original language is apparently impossible to resolve, and de Chirico's 1928 letter to Scheiwiller seems to suggest a simultaneous drafting in both French and Italian: yet another duplication, as if a French de Chirico were reflected in his Italian counterpart, matching the doubling between author and character. The few mentions in the Italian literature were amplified in introductions to reissues of the book by Giorgio Manganelli (1971) and Aldo Paladini (1972). Now, in light of this brief historical and critical context, let's consider how to read *Hebdomeros*.

When Jean Cocteau wrote *Le Mystère laïc*, in 1928, he produced certainly one of the most intimate and profound monographs on the artist. He stated: "Picasso and de Chirico paralyze the public, who read upon Picasso's still lifes: *Keep Out*, and on de Chirico's streets: *Do Not Enter – Wrong Way*." De Chirico, true enough, prevents viewers and readers from entering his work. The construction of mystery cannot be explained if it is to work; indeed, access must be forbidden. He does all he can do to deny any easy, direct perusal of both his paintings and his writings. But that doesn't mean that this admirable construction is senseless or devoid of order. *Hebdomeros* is an uninterrupted sequence that abounds with visions, associations, and references which challenge the reader. The continuous flow, the stream of consciousness, is not all that dissimilar from Joyce's in *Ulysses*. Nino Frank's review provides a clear connection between the two works. Indeed, *Hebdomeros* is a *Ulysses*, its story the tale of a journey through time and ideas, retracing, step by step, a path of life, understanding, and a deepening self-knowledge.

Let us begin by considering the name of the protagonist, which gives the book its title. It is the product of one of those plays on words that so fascinated de Chirico and his brother, Alberto Savinio. Like so many other elements of their culture, the name found its roots in their friendship and admiration for Apollinaire, an origin story like that which fertilized the birth of surrealism. Here we find an abundance of composite, polysemous terms, rich in both meanings and ambiguity, that attribute multiple, anamorphic, and occasionally contradictory characteristics to the characters, echoing the ambiguity of life and the world. The very name Apollinaire is a pseudonym that contains the name Apollo and means "sacred to Apollo." In his writings, the French poet used combinations of Greek names, such as for the protagonist of his autobiographical poem *The Poet Assassinated*, Croniamantal, the "diviner of time." Hebdomeros is a combination of Hebdomagetis (lord of the seventh day) or Hebdomagenis (born on the seventh day), both epithets of Apollo, with the suffix Eros, meaning "lover of Apollo." But in de Chirico's polysemous pun, one can also extrapolate the name Omeros, translating it as "the Seventh Homer," or "the Homer of the Seventh Day." Apollo-Homer-de Chirico-Ulysses: a multifaceted, chimerical autobiographical character, deeply rooted in the author's native Greece.

Let us now outline the novel's complex narrative rhythm, albeit at the risk of oversimplification. The story begins with a prologue of sorts and continues with childhood and youth in Greece; this first part ends with the words "He wanted only to flee." This is followed by passage to Italy and Germany, in turn concluding with the phrase "Hebdomeros had to flee." Flight is thus semantically understood as a transition from one phase of life to another, and from one chapter of the narrative to another, clearly marked by movement from one city and country to another (it is worth noting that de Chirico, from his birth until 1929, lived in Volos and Athens, Munich, Milan, Florence, Paris, Ferrara, Rome, and Paris again). The narrative continues with the complicated time in Italy, first in Milan and then in Florence, where in the autumn of 1910, metaphysics was born (here he mentions elements of one of his early Böcklin-inspired paintings from the spring-summer of 1910, *Serenata*). The Paris period, in the second half of the book, begins when the protagonist arrives in a metropolis of almost eight million people: memories from his more recent stays, between 1925 and 1929, blend with visions from his first stay as a young man, from 1911 to 1915, along with echoes of Ferrara and Rome, in a kind of amalgamation where images of his paintings become increasingly frequent and aesthetic discussions more explicit and less cryptically prophetic.

If this is the general course of the narrative, de Chirico is very careful, as Cocteau said, to post NO ENTRY signs to prevent readers from accessing his narrative rhythm too easily. Thus, he inserts in unexpected locations memories from other periods, elusive meditations, and interpretive traps to dismantle the general order he himself has given the story; he also removes pauses between one narrative phase and another, making the overarching narrative tapestry seemingly impossible to disentangle. The book teems with such disorienting insertions, of varying length and importance. One particularly explicit and integral insertion is found at the end of the novel, where he returns to an evocation of his father, his childhood, Athens and Volos, his family's deepest roots: right in the heart of the narrative, he unleashes, like a bolt of lightning, an unexpected flashback. This is also a way for de Chirico to connect his experiences in a circular system, in a Nietzschean "eternal return," with no hierarchy in terms of importance or chronology. The final pages, in fact, are devoted to the memory of the advent of metaphysics (which he recounts in more realist terms in his memoir, which he published in 1962): stomach discomfort, the month of September, the evocation of Nietzsche, eternity, time, etc.

The final pages are also a lyrical digression about Ferrara ("he knew them well, those interminable afternoons in the map room"), Athens ("at the gates of oriental cities"), Apollinaire ("if in dark and sordid streets the furious commoners stoned thy son," an allusion to *The Poet Assassinated*), and Zarathustra ("thou, visible to myself alone, thou whose glance speaks to me of immortality!"). These are his most intense and profound points of reference. The novel concludes with an affectionate homage to his beloved brother ("one day, O brother ... "), where he freely quotes the "Hamletic" words of his first youthful text, published in the *Almanac* of the magazine *Coenobium* in 1910: "Have you ever thought of my death? Have you ever thought of the death of my death?" The book closes with a cameo, with a cinematic zoom on the protagonist: the image of Hebdomeros in a melancholy pose, a blend of his first metaphysical portrait, *Portrait de l'artiste par lui-même* (1910–1911), with the Nietzschean epigraph "Et quid amabo nisi quod rerum metaphysica est?" (And what shall I love, if not the metaphysics of things?) and, as we shall shortly see, a portrait of Ernest Renan. Hebdomeros rests his chin in his hand, his elbow propped upon a ruin, against the backdrop of the Aegean Sea with a procession of islands sailing by (an allusion to Delos, the island of Apollo and Diana, or to the "wandering islands" of the Argonauts in the narration of Apollonius of Rhodes) and birds in flight. The novel ends with ellipses, exactly as it began, a sign of the eternal circularity of life and death, with no beginning or end.

If this general guide helps us gain access to the book's labyrinthine plotlines, without necessarily leading us to a safe exit, it should also be noted that what distinguishes de Chirico from Breton and other surrealist writers is his rich array of literary and museological references. De Chirico's refined and indeed Babelic literary culture, at once dense and stretched practically to the breaking point, lines up with his personal choices of eccentric, unexpected eclecticism, skewed toward the strange, the rare, and the mysterious. On one hand, such preferences seem to align with those professed by Breton: Lautréamont, Nerval, Rimbaud, Poe, De Quincey, who, as we have seen, were recognized by de Chirico's French reviewers at the time and, indeed, formed part of the surrealist experimental laboratory. But on the other hand, we should not forget that their initial consideration stemmed from the mystical and esoteric recommendations of de Chirico's great poet friend Apollinaire. It was he who recommended readings that marked de Chirico so deeply, not the younger Breton (who also learned of them through his parallel friendship with Apollinaire). Indeed, de Chirico indirectly quotes Apollinaire several times in *Hebdomeros*: though once almost explicitly, referring to summer as "that season which a great poet termed *violent*," from the poem "La jolie rousse," in the collection *Calligrammes*; another time evoking the story of *The Poet Assassinated*, associating it with the theme of the "Monomachos," or gladiator.[9]

While the surrealists avoided direct citations, instead preferring the raw expression of a psyche free to express itself without intermediaries, de Chirico built a labyrinth of citations and references atop his psychic and dream-like associations. It was precisely this ability to unite dreams with literature, and with universal culture and personal history and interests, that so fascinated Jorge Luis Borges, as we shall soon see. In addition, this structure echoes the theme of the labyrinth itself, to which de Chirico alludes in his work, by way of Ariadne, who is closely bound up with melancholy.

De Chirico explicitly mentions several writers in *Hebdomeros* (Homer, Byron, Renan), while he makes cryptic but specific references to such writers as Apollinaire, Dante, Leopardi, Verne, Savinio, and Cocteau.[10] He alludes to painters and works by Böcklin, Klinger, Brouillet, Segantini, and Lorrain.[11] The only artist he directly cites is André Brouillet, but he distorts the name to Brouillé, so no critic has yet identified the painting in question, *Renan in Front of the Parthenon* (de Chirico sees Renan as nearly a portrait of himself, associating the background of the Parthenon with the "far-off landscape of factories and smoking chimneys" in the nearby Gazi district of Athens).[12] Likewise, no one has discussed Renan's influence on de Chirico's intellect. Renan's prayer at the Acropolis (*Prière que je fis sur l'Acropole quand je fus arrivé à en comprendre la parfaite beauté*) is one of the most intense declarations of philhellenism in Western culture, and its presence here offers a gauge of how deeply de Chirico felt tied to his Greek origins, the intellectual matrix that marked his spirit during his childhood and youth in Volos and Athens, and all phases of his painting. When he returned to Athens in 1973—for the first time since leaving, at eighteen, in 1906—the first words he uttered upon disembarking, in an elegant Greek still clearly marked by the accent of his native city, were: "I will fall to the ground and weep."[13]

The themes and images of de Chirico's paintings, especially from 1925 to 1929, weave in and out of the brilliant visual apparatus upon which the book is built. *Interno metafisico – L'après-midi d'été* (1925), *La maison aux volets verts* (1926), and *Périclès* (1926) are just some of the paintings described in the novel, either precisely or with narrative variations. Archaeologists, gladiators, rooms inhabited by forests, temples, and "the making of trophies" are scattered throughout the book. There are also allusions to his earlier paintings, from the early Böcklin-inspired works to a *Roman Villa* (1922) and metaphysical works inhabited by mysterious characters and unsettling shadows.

As has frequently been noted, *Hebdomeros* is a visual novel. Every de Chirico–esque image is laden with philosophical, literary, mnemonic, and allusive references: the scenes are not simply paintings for their own sake, autonomous or aesthetic descriptions, or lyrical expressions. De Chirico's complex thought process was absolutely original within contemporary art, as he drew anew upon psyche and memory, dreams and imagination, marking a radical transition from traditional forms to a new system of meaning. De Chirico's image becomes the concept itself, capable of evoking, like an oracle, the dark truths of thought and reality. This results in an extrasensory ability to express thought directly through his painted images. In literature, he managed to develop something similar, and it was apparently unprecedented: the story unfolds not in concatenated narratives but in images that emerge like enigmatic icebergs from an ocean; the story is the journey—the voyage—and it is one with the character. While Joyce works with the word as a psychic signifier in *Ulysses*, de Chirico constructs an image generated directly from the psyche; however, like Joyce, he uses literary and visual culture in the broadest and most eclectic sense, as a bridge between man and the world, between singular events and the expanse of history.

In the final analysis, de Chirico evokes images whose ambiguity leads us into a spiral of dreams, at the bottom of which lies the meaning, like an octopus coiled on a seabed. As a midwife, the author guides us on the "initiatic" journey: "be methodical, don't waste your strength; when you have found a sign, turn it around and around, look at it from the front and from the side, take a three-quarter view and a foreshortened view; remove it and note what form the memory of its appearance takes in its place; observe from which angle it looks like a horse, and from which like the molding on your ceiling; see when it suggests the aspect of a ladder, or a plumed helmet; in which position it resembles Africa, which itself resembles a large heart." He resurrects the gods, ambiguously but lightly, ironically actualizing them in the modern world: "Hebdomeros could not share the opinion of those skeptics who considered that all this was make-believe and that centaurs had never existed, any more than fauns, sirens, and tritons. As if to prove the contrary, they were all at the door, pawing the ground and chasing with great swishes of their tails the flies which clung obstinately to their twitching flanks." De Chirico has the power of evocation necessary to bring to life ancient Greece, the mother of Western thought, as if centuries had not passed. Mount Pelion, in whose shadow he was born, was the homeland of centaurs and Argonauts; Athens, the center of antiquity, where he came of age and first encountered Nietzsche, who had rediscovered the profound meaning of Greece. His Hellenic childhood and youth are the primeval, archetypal foundation upon which his extraordinary innovation in modern art and literature rests.

The best way for a reader to approach the text of *Hebdomeros* is certainly to identify with a devotee of Apollo, the god of the sun, who goes to the Pythia at Delphi to hear the oracle's voice. It may seem difficult, but de Chirico provides all the tools. In his nonsense, which unites the origin of ancestral times with the future, he inscribes his imagination, fertilized by the knowingness of the oracle: "A magic word shone in the air like the cross of Constantine and multiplied itself in space to the edge of the horizon like the ads for a toothpaste: *Delphoï! Delphoï!*" This method is no more eccentric than the demands of many avant-garde authors, from Yeats and Joyce to Breton and Apollinaire and Virginia Woolf.

In conclusion, I would like to propose a single but significant example of the influence *Hebdomeros* had on world literature.[14] Jorge Luis Borges has often been associated with de Chirico, as if they were brothers in their visions. They have been paired for their labyrinths and scorched images of shadows and architecture. In 1940, Borges, together with Silvina Ocampo and Adolfo Bioy Casares, published *Antología de la literatura fantástica* (*The Book of Fantasy*), a collection of stories on the theme of the fantastic, the "metaphysical," from every era. De Chirico is absent from this anthology, as is Gérard de Nerval. But de Chirico's spirit lurks like an unnamed deity: it was he who invented the temporal short circuit and enigmatic signs that pervade their stories, from Borges's *The Aleph* to Bioy Casares's *The Invention of Morel*. The connection was direct: Ocampo had studied drawing in Paris with de Chirico, and his imagination struck her like lightning. Borges had the opportunity to read *Hebdomeros* and referenced it several times in some of his most mysterious stories, particularly *Fictions* and *The Aleph*, whose dreamlike rhythms often echo that of *Hebdomeros*. One unequivocal example is in Borges's *The Writing of the God*: the protagonist discovers in the mystery contained in the jaguar's spotted skin the key to the enigmatic formula devised by the creator god to save the world from "many calamities and ruins"; de Chirico speaks in *Hebdomeros* of "what is enigmatic about ... the spotted skin of the leopard," linking it to the enigma of life and death, "ghosts foretelling disasters to come." Too much to be a coincidence. Similarly, the environments and metaphysical cities described in *The Immortal* and other stories clearly derive from those imagined by *Hebdomeros*, which, as Borges knew, partly drew on Nerval's *Aurélia*. We cannot dwell here on the many literal similarities—that would be another essay entirely. Let us simply end here with a magnificent poem composed by Silvina Ocampo, which has been strangely unknown in de Chirico studies and demonstrates the inner reflection on de Chirico among this literary group:[15]

Epistle to Giorgio de Chirico

Giorgio de Chirico, I was your student.
I remember the Greek profile and the apple,
the Parisian sky in the window
where you dreamed of space and the column.

While I painted impetuously,
in silence, attentively, its gaze
frightened me in its imprisoned face;
Giorgio de Chirico, you were patient.

And I remember, in your paintings, with a plaster cast,
fish whose blood did not stain:
you, to surprise me, would touch them.
I burst out laughing. Forgive me for this.

In the tragic domain of the sea
in your paintings, the blue wind is silent,
and in a flash, seen on the beach
are two horses with triangular fury.

The moving truck with mirrors,
the furniture crowding the desert,
the half-open window, with shadows,
over the mystical ardor of reflections,

of those inhabitants of my dream,
of those gladiators in the arena,
of the girl with the bow on the serene
pathetic street, you are the master.

Europe is bleeding; so it is the war
with the foliage of explosions
that has destroyed tender hearts,
the children, the hearths, and the land.

But the world in your paintings, admirable,
which sought the building and the molding
and disdained the sweetness of the tree,
remains in time, irrevocable.

The wings of paper, the red walls,
the dark cathedral, the sad swan,
what you have not yet painted exists for me
with your images in my eyes.

The black, the ocher, and the blue – the mystery
of the air in your paintings – have followed me
with brilliance in life. Reality has promised
to accept its captivity.

The centaurea is denser, more open;
the seasons hear more secrets,
raising their arms, high, still;
there are sounds of the sea at every door.

Giorgio de Chirico in an arcane dream
spoke to a dead man in the shadow of the laurel:
"Oh Piranesi, the noble capital
moves more deeply, without flowers, than a summer.

I will not invoke leaves or branches
to paint lasting landscapes;
I will not invoke real men:
I want the building's wall in flames,

the man like a stick on the ground,
the spiders with trembling shadows,
the mask, the defined foam,
the tormented shapes in the sky."

In writing one of the key novels of the twentieth century, de Chirico deliberately sealed it in a secret niche, accessible to only a few. Perhaps the time has come to recognize its role, its profound beauty, and its importance.

Amorgos, August 2019

Notes

1   The subtitle of the first edition, *Le peintre et son génie chez l'écrivain*, which disappears in later editions, indicates de Chirico's intention to challenge the surrealists.

2   See Fabio Benzi, *Giorgio de Chirico: Life and Paintings* (New York: Rizzoli Electa, 2023), chap. 19–20.

3   Pierre Cabanne, *Entretiens avec Marcel Duchamp* (Paris: Pierre Belfond, 1967).

4   In a letter dated July 21, 1928, de Chirico wrote to the Italian publisher Giovanni Scheiwiller: "I am finishing a very important book; it is a kind of sequel to the Metaphysical tales, two of which have already appeared in Waldemar George's book. The book's title is *Hebdomeros*. I am writing it in Italian and translating it into French myself as I go; the French version will be published by a local publisher. Would you like to publish the Italian version?" De Chirico, *Lettere 1909–1929*, ed. Elena Pontiggia (Milan: Silvana Editoriale, 2018), p. 409. Waldemar George's book is *Chirico: Avec des fragments littéraires de l'artiste* (Paris: Éditions des Chroniques du Jour, 1928).

5   See Louis Aragon, *La peinture au défi*. Exh. cat. (Paris: Galerie Goemans, 1930). In a risky contortion, Aragon acknowledges de Chirico's brilliance but sycophantically follows the surrealist line in undermining his recent painting: "The painter's genius today expresses itself wonderfully through writing, when he abandons the tricks and delights of painting and relies on intellect rather than craft." Aragon fails to realize that the book is a literary representation of the very painting he disparages.

6   James Thrall Soby to Alfred Barr, letter dated February 9, 1943. JTS Papers, The Museum of Modern Art Archives, New York.

7   Interview by Pierre Lagarde, "M. de Chirico, peintre prédit et souhait le triomphe du modernisme," *Comoedia*, December 12, 1927.

8   De Chirico, "Max Klinger," *Il Convegno* 10, 1920.

9   The theme of the gladiator is addressed in de Chirico's commemoration of Apollinaire's life and in *Hebdomeros* and his paintings, in an intimate homage to the poet. "The phalanx is not broken" by death. "What he gave us, we will repay." De Chirico, "Guillaume Apollinaire," *Ars Nova* 2, 1918. De Chirico saw himself and Apollinaire as two gladiators beyond time, united by their understanding of the absolute. In 1930, he again paid homage to Apollinaire by illustrating *Calligrammes* with a series of lithographs.

10 There are many references to Leopardi: to *The Song of the Great Wild Rooster*, a phrase that de Chirico slightly modifies, turning it from the already strange original Chaldean-qua-cabalistic language into a magical phrase; to *Zibaldone*, recalled in the beginning of the novel; and to the

poem "Night Song of a Wandering Shepherd in Asia." Dante is evoked through the figure of the greyhound; Verne through "passengers in a highly advanced submarine …"; Cocteau by the image of a fatal accident from *Le Mystère laïc* ("horrible disasters, cars smashed to smithereens and men cut to pieces").

11 Böcklin is mentioned at several points, starting with specific memories of Basel; Klinger via the title of his engraving *In flagranti* and a painting depicting the crucifixion; Segantini via the painting *Le due madri* (The Two Mothers); Lorrain via the painting of Mercury described on p. 122.

12 See Benzi, *Giorgio de Chirico: Life and Paintings.*

13 De Chirico to Angelos Delivorrias, director of the Benaki Museum; re-layed to the author by the Athenian artist Alekos Levidis.

14 Another example, in Italian literature, can be found in Italo Calvino's *Invisible Cities* (1972), mindful of both Borges and de Chirico.

15 First published in Silvina Ocampo, *Poemas de amor desesperado* (Buenos Aires: Editorial Sudamericana, 1949). Its writing dates to World War II ("Europe is bleeding"). Ocampo was a close friend of Borges's and was married to Bioy Casares.

Hebdomeros

Giorgio de Chirico

. . . .

... and then began the visit to that strange building located in an austerely respectable but by no means dismal street. Seen from outside, the building made one think of a German consulate in Melbourne. Large shops took up the whole ground floor. Though it was neither a Sunday nor a holiday the shops were closed at the time, which gave to this portion of the street a weary, melancholy air, a particular desolation, that dreary atmosphere one associates with Anglo-Saxon towns on Sundays. A faint smell of docks hung in the air, the indefinable and highly suggestive odor given off by warehouses adjoining the wharves in a port. The idea that the building resembled a German consulate in Melbourne was a purely personal one of Hebdomeros's, and when he spoke about it to his friends they smiled and said they found the comparison *odd*, but they immediately dropped the subject and went on to talk about something else. Hebdomeros concluded from this that perhaps they had not really understood what he meant, and he reflected on the difficulty of making oneself understood when one's thoughts reached a certain height or depth. "It's strange," Hebdomeros was thinking, "as for me, the very idea that something had escaped my understanding would keep me awake at nights, whereas people in general are not in the least perturbed when they see or read or hear things they find completely obscure." They began to climb the stairs, which were very wide and made throughout of varnished wood; running up the middle was a carpet; at the foot of the stairs on a little Doric column carved out of oak and joined to the end of the banister stood a polychrome statue, also carved in wood, representing a Californian Negro with his hands stretched above his head, holding aloft a gas lamp whose burner had an asbestos mantle over it. Hebdomeros felt as though he were going upstairs to visit a dentist, or a doctor specializing in venereal diseases; this perturbed him a little, and he felt the onset of something like the colic; he tried to fight down this uneasiness by reminding himself he was not alone, that two of his friends were with him—strong, athletic fellows carrying automatics with spare magazines in the pockets of their trousers. When they saw they were coming to the floor which they had been told had a history of being haunted by strange apparitions, they slowed down and began to climb on tiptoe, looking more warily around them. They stayed abreast of one another but moved apart a little so they could get downstairs quickly and freely, should they encounter a particularly strange kind of apparition. At that moment Hebdomeros thought of his childhood dreams; in a state of anguish he would be climbing a staircase bathed in a dim light, a staircase made of varnished wood with a thick carpet in the middle which muffled his footsteps (as it so happens, his shoes rarely squeaked even outside his dreams for he had them made to measure by a shoemaker named Perpignani, known throughout the town for the high quality of his leather; Hebdomeros's father, on the other hand, was hopeless when it came to buying shoes; his shoes made a horrible noise, as if he were crushing bags of nuts at every step). Then came the apparition of the bear, the frightening, relentless bear that follows you on the stairs and along the corridors, its head lowered, and looking as if its thoughts were elsewhere; the headlong flight through rooms with complicated exits, the leap through the window into empty space (suicide in a dream) and the gliding descent, like those condor-men Leonardo drew for amusement among his catapults and anatomical fragments. It was a dream which always foretold trouble, especially sickness.

"Here we are!" said Hebdomeros, throwing his arms out in front of his companions, in the classic pose of a captain prudently halting the charge of his men. They were coming to the threshold of a vast, high-ceilinged room, decorated in the style of 1880; the lighting and general atmosphere of this room, which was completely bare of furniture, reminded one of the gaming rooms at Monte Carlo; in a corner two gladiators wearing diving helmets were practicing half-heartedly, watched by a bored instructor, a retired gladiator with eyes like a vulture and a body covered with scars. "*Gladiators!* There's an enigma in that word," said Hebdomeros, speaking in a low voice to the younger of his companions. And he thought of the music halls whose brightly lit ceilings conjure up visions of Dante's paradise; he also thought of those afternoons in Rome, when the games would be over for the day and the sun sinking lower in the sky, the immense canopy over the arena augmenting the evening shadows, and smells floating up from the sawdust and blood-soaked sand ...

Vision of Rome, when the world was young,
Anguish at nightfall, a sailor's song.

More of those upholstered doors and short, deserted corridors, and then suddenly: *Society! Go out in the world. Live the life of a socialite. Social etiquette. How to behave. Invitation card.* R.S.V.P. (répondez s'il vous plaît). P.D. (personal delivery). P.T.O. (please turn over). In a corner of the drawing room stood an enormous grand piano with its top up; without standing on tiptoe you could see its complicated entrails and clear-cut internal anatomy; but you could easily imagine what a catastrophe it would have been if one of those chandeliers laden with pink and blue wax candles had fallen into the piano with all the candles lit. What a disaster in the myelogenous abyss! With the wax running down the steel strings, stretched taut like Ulysses's bow, and hindering the precise working of the little felt-covered hammers. "Better not think about it," said Hebdomeros, turning to his companions; then all three of them, holding hands as though in the face of danger, looked silently and intently at the astonishing scene; they imagined they were passengers in a highly advanced submarine, looking through the portholes and watching unobserved the mysterious plant and animal life of the deep. For that matter, the scene before them really did have an underwater quality to it. It reminded one of a large aquarium, if only on account of the diffused light which eliminated all the shadows. A strange, inexplicable silence lay over the whole scene: that pianist sitting at his instrument and playing *without making a sound*, that pianist you didn't really see, as there was nothing about him that deserved to be seen, and those characters in a drama, moving around the piano with cups of coffee in their hands, making the gestures and movements of athletes jumping in slow-motion films; all these people lived in a world of their own, a world apart; *they knew nothing about anything*; they had never heard of the war in Transvaal or the disaster in Martinique; they did not recognize you, for they had never met you; nothing could disturb them or have any hold over them, neither prussic acid nor a stiletto nor an armor-piercing bullet. If a *rebel* (let's call him that) had had a mind to light the fuse of an infernal machine, the hundred pounds of lyddite in it would have burned away slowly, hissing like damp logs. It was enough to make you despair. Hebdomeros held that it was the effect of the environment, of the *atmosphere*, and he knew no way of altering anything about it; the only thing to do was to live and let live. But—*that is the question*[1]—were they really alive? ... It would have been very difficult to give a reply, especially just like that, right away, without devoting several nights of deep meditation to the question, as Hebdomeros always did when his mind was haunted by a complicated problem.

Moreover, he was afraid of opening a discussion with his friends on the eternal questions: What is life? What

---

1   In English in the original. (Translator's note)

is death? Is life possible on another planet? Do you believe in metempsychosis, in the immortality of the soul, in the violability of the laws of nature, in ghosts foretelling disasters to come, in the subconscious of dogs, in the dreams of owls, in what is enigmatic about cicadas, quail's heads, and the spotted skin of the leopard? He hated discussions of this kind, even though deep down he felt instinctively attracted to the enigmatic element in all things, animate and inanimate. But misgivings were aroused in him by other people, those who discussed things with him; he abhorred their high opinion of themselves, their rancor, their hysteria; he had no wish to awaken complex feelings in his friends; he also shrank from their admiration; all such exclamations as: *Great! Marvelous! Wonderful!* gave him little or no satisfaction and eventually irritated him. He was only happy when nobody took the slightest notice of him; to be dressed like everybody else, to attract no attention, never to feel others' glances piercing his back or sides, even if they were kindly glances. Or else, yes, he would have liked people to pay attention to him but *in a totally different way*. Yes, he would have liked that: to have all the advantages and satisfaction of being famous but with none of the bother. The life of a sybarite, if you will!

Ex.: The broken vase was very valuable.

Ex.: The closed door would not budge.

Let's take the example of the broken vase. Though it was widely believed he was a child-martyr whose cruel mother gave him a beating on the slightest pretext, this was completely untrue, as could easily be seen at that moment, the whole family being gathered together in the middle of the dining room around the broken remains of their cherished vase from Rhodes, which had stood on the buffet for ninety-two years. With the palms of their hands resting on their bent knees and their elbows sticking out as though they were sitting on invisible stools, the seven members of the family stared down at the whitish fragments. But nobody moved, nobody *accused him*. They were staring with the intent interest of archaeologists watching a statue being unearthed, or of paleontologists eagerly looking at a fossil just brought to light by the pick.

They were talking of gluing the pieces together again, and each was putting in his word. Some said they knew of expert craftsmen who did this kind of work so perfectly that afterward you couldn't see any sign of the break. The lady of the house (the woman accused by the whole district of being a terror to young Achilles) was the least impressed of all; she was the first to break the spell they were under as they gazed. Achilles's brother was of the opinion that it was the way the pieces were scattered on the floor which was largely responsible for hypnotizing the seven members of the family. And it was true that the pieces were arranged in the form of a trapezoid, like a well-known constellation; the idea of the sky being turned upside down had mesmerized these good folk, to the extent of immobilizing them, and when all was said and done—apart from the fact they were looking down instead of looking up—at that moment they were the worthy colleagues of those early Chaldean or Babylonian astronomers who kept watch through the fine summer nights, lying out on terraces with their heads turned up toward the stars. But no one ever went into the adjoining room. Here was the place of the buffet, the silver teapot and the dread of the great black cockroaches in the depths of the empty pots. It had never occurred to Hebdomeros to associate the idea of cockroaches and the idea of fish, but the two words *great* and *black* reminded him of a poignant scene, half-Homeric, half-Byronic, which he had once briefly witnessed toward evening on the rocky shores of an arid island. This scene had caused Hebdomeros acute disappointment, followed soon after by shame. The sea was smooth, perfectly mirroring the sky in the light of the setting sun. Now and then, with clockwork regularity, a long wave began to form at some distance from the shore, swelling up and gathering speed, then crashing headlong against the shore with the noise of a thunderclap sliced in two. Between one wave and the next there was absolute silence and calm. This was the setting in which Hebdomeros heard for the first time the entreaty of the fisherman's wife. At first he thought her husband had already set out in his boat toward the open sea, and he could not help taking the words of the song as a bad omen for the fishermen, as something which sooner or later would bring down misfortune on these men, constantly exposed as they were to the dangers of storms:

Let my arms be your oars and my tresses your ropes,
For the great black fishes might swallow you up
In the fathomless depths of the sea.

Fortunately, on this occasion his anguish was short-lived, for a few moments later he caught sight of the husband, quietly mending his nets at his fisherman's hut some thirty steps from there. A gust of wind had pushed the door open, exposing him to this sight. This episode made Hebdomeros feel a vague sadness in his heart, mingled with a sense of disappointment. Yet he should have been glad at the thought that the fisherman, instead of being devoured by the great black fish in the fathomless depths of the sea, was quietly mending his nets on the doorstep of his hut. But such is human nature: we hunger for tragedy and catastrophes. We are always disappointed when we come upon a crowd of people in the street and find that it's only a ring of bystanders around a hawker selling fountain pens, whereas from a distance we had been imagining horrible disasters, cars smashed to smithereens and men cut to pieces; or again, when we see two angry people hurling violent insults at each other, then settling their quarrel without coming to blows and offering us one of those magnificent fist fights, so lavishly provided by American films and so rare, alas!—but no wonder—in French ones. Hebdomeros thought of all this as he examined and analyzed his state of mind; he ended by being ashamed of his feelings and as he made his way to the hotel for his evening meal he was blushing like a pure young girl who, chasing a playful butterfly as it flutters behind a bush, suddenly comes upon a male adult with his trousers down, squatting to satisfy a need as natural as it was urgent.

In the little garden of the hotel, strewn with small polished stones, it was a cheerless dinner they had together, the two men with the goatee beards, wearing crumpled, rather dirty, white linen waistcoats with elaborate charms hanging from their watch chains. One of them was saying that sometimes he woke up hungry during the night, so he had taken to having a large bowl of milk set out on the bedside table by his maid when she came to turn back the sheets in the evening; when he got into bed he took up the bowl, raising it as though to pour a libation, then drank it down at one gulp before going to sleep. The other man who, though older, was even more brutish, was telling how on summer nights when the town was almost deserted (its inhabitants having gone to the seaside or the country to escape from the midsummer heat) he would walk down the avenue des Citronniers at about three in the morning with two young ladies of easy virtue, one on each arm. Hebdomeros, as he half listened to them talking, was trying to recall a scene which remained blurred in his mind's eye. He could vaguely recollect a room which had no windows facing the sea; its only opening was toward the north, so that the room was lit like an artist's studio, and through this opening could be seen far in the distance a part of that long mountain whose other side sloped down toward the gulf; nearer at hand you could see trees, especially pine trees. The fierce winds which often blew from the sea had twisted them into the would-be aesthetic poses of exotic dancers; this made a rather curious contrast at that moment with the absolute stillness which lay over everything. In the bright light of that fine October day it was as though the hapless trees were racked by the torture of a never-ending storm, while behind them to the north (the side diametrically opposite the sea) the horizon shone with all the purity of a Swiss landscape. This made Hebdomeros think of Basel and of the bridges over the Rhine, whose emerald waters rush along in a torrent. Still further off in the distance majestic mountains rose high, with their snow-capped peaks sparkling in the sunshine. Here was the site of the famous caves inhabited by demigods who, when young, were warlike and boastful but who later, as their lives wore on and the time for them to cross the threshold into the blissful kingdom of Life Eternal drew near, turned into sages and poets and then, with the nonchalance of Platonic boy-lovers, taught their grandsons the art of making medicines by grinding bitter plants and the art of tuning the huge lyre, massive and heavy as a miniaturized cathedral. Though autumn had stripped bare the century-old trees, this whole vast horizon spoke of everlasting life.

Before the shrines in which the sacred weapons of Hercules moldered and rusted away under sacrosanct tombstones bearded warriors of flawless profiles and virile beauty stood guard. Along the brick walls on the side the sun's rays never reached, ivy climbed and green moss grew. It was the season when Valtadore took the winter carpets out of their boxes and shook off the naphthalene that covered them …

Winds on shore
The weather fine
Evening storms
Of summertime.

It was gone now, the burning summer, with dinners on the beach. Hebdomeros recalled those dinners whose main dish was rotting red mullet which poisoned the bathers, causing them to writhe all night in the throes of colic as they lay in their hotel rooms on sheets made hot by the midsummer heat, in a stifling atmosphere that stank of dirty toilets and linoleum; through the open window came the sound of the waves as they broke at regular intervals on the shore, somewhere out there in the darkness.

It was time to get up and go out; this thought had been nagging at Hebdomeros for some time. The peacocks, as they trailed their ocellated tails under the trees of the wild garden, gave heartrending cries which conveyed the very peculiar *quality* of the facade of this old-fashioned villa whose long veranda was crammed with plants and artificial flowers. So now the great problem was to get out. There are times when this can be done without difficulty; at a party, for example, when everyone is talking and gesticulating, when the guests are going from one room to another, absorbed by the need to be clever and round off brilliantly the conversations they have begun; in that case it is child's play to slip past the guests and take French leave; on the other hand there are times when this is much more difficult to do; that was what Hebdomeros was thinking as he stood in the middle of the room, surrounded by all those fifty-year-old prostitutes, looking as stern as unyielding Areopagites, who were sitting with their Herculean arms folded on their enlarged breasts, like wrestlers posing for a photographer. And their hostile eyes converged on him like the guns of a squadron on an enemy's coastal fort. It would have needed courage that no human being could have summoned to rise and escape from this infernal, watchful circle. That is why Hebdomeros preferred to remain, feigning interest in all the pictures and *objets d'art*, though they were of very indifferent quality and he had known them by heart since he was a child. And he yielded to the delight of reliving a bygone hour: twilight, gardens draped in the evening mist; artillery barracks, an earthquake, a "seismic disturbance," as the newspapers put it. The whole population of the district was spending the night in the open; mattresses thrown out of the windows and arranged in the main square around the statue of the tailcoated politician holding a stone scroll on which the sculptor had engraved his name and the date of the work. Some said that a comet was coming and with it the end of the world, as predicted in the books of astrology. Years of one's youth, of serenades by the foot of those necropolises, so white in the moonlight!—and those truly extraordinary nights when flowers thrown into the air fell thick and fast, and the solitary shores awash with the countless offerings of a sea whose every wave bore thousands and thousands of roses. And now, after all that, to end up in this huge glass house, seeking a fugitive ideal in the midst of so many fellow sufferers. This, then, was why he spent whole nights sitting up in bed, his head in his hands, while on the table, between his pipe and tobacco pouch, the candle deformed by dripping wax, burned down. But at such moments it sometimes happened that the back wall opened up like a theater curtain and visions appeared, sometimes terrifying, sometimes sublime or enchanting: there would be the ocean in a storm, with hideous gnomes leering and making threatening gestures on the foaming crests of the waves; and sometimes also you would see a spring landscape of astonishing poetry and peacefulness: green, gentle slopes rising on either side of a path whose edges were shaded by almond trees in blossom; along the path slowly walked a woman dressed all in white, her face thoughtful and serious. "But it's nothing," said Hebdomeros, "compared to what that town was like on summer nights." It was Parthenonized, pedagogized, and ephebogogized, this fairly low but well-proportioned building, looking for all the world like an enormous toy which, after several failures, had been finally placed in position. Its front faced south and so toward the sea; its stern was to the north, and the children came to lean over it, those children who loved to daydream, for the north attracted them more than the other cardinal points; later they would feel the pull of the west as well, but for the moment, only the north existed for them. At noon in those transitional seasons, autumn and spring, the sky was as blue as a piece of taut paper; there was no lighter area near the horizon; it was blue all over from top to bottom; a veritable ceiling stretching over the town. On those days of supreme happiness, the sense of north, south, east, and west—all sense of direction, in fact—was lost to these young people, these virgin athletes and adolescent gymnasts at practice running on the shining tracks. Sometimes the solid silver cups and laurel crowns were carried off by girls who sped over the arena like does with feet of bronze. When that happened, the children and the youths enjoyed equal status, and those who at other times dreamed of the north forgot their reveries. Yet, there was no doubt about it: all these young people were living through one of the most moving hours of their lives. The youths already old enough to practice in the palaestra, or the children still playing at making sand castles or setting traps baited with black olives for the whistling blackbirds—all of them would have been called, sooner or later, to govern public affairs or to take sword in hand to defend the sacred soil of their motherland; or else to trade and build, or make sculptures of warriors and great politicians so that their effigies, naked or clothed according to the fashion of the day, would stand in the peaceful shade of the squares, where the wet nurses gathered with their babes.

Or again, they might have been called upon to explore far-off lands, retiring at night into wagons fitted up as traveling homes and sleeping there, tired from the day's hunting, to the cries of hyenas and jackals. Or yet again, they would have traded with neighboring lands, would have bought and sold merchandise in corded bales, every one of the same shape and as alike one another as twins. Yes, there was no doubt about it: all these young people were living in an *eternal present*. Henceforth it was only a matter of hours, for Nature, wise in all she does (so people say, at least), would not have let such intense, such delicately bred happiness last too long, since too much happiness, like too much sorrow, could have weakened the moral fiber of these sensitive, impulsive young people. Only in the rest of the city was Sunday, the day of rest, rather less cheerful. But in this stronghold of the pure in heart there was undiminished joy as the workmen feverishly strove to have everything ready for the appointed day. What joyous songs of men happily at work! And it was work, regular daily work, which prevented all their minds, obsessed as they were by the highest metaphysical speculations, from the depths of despair. Even far into the night, as the whole city lay sleeping under the star-filled sky, the joyful sound of their work resounded through the interior cloisters. Everything was progressing, advancing, going forward by leaps and bounds, until it all led up to that memorable afternoon (for they had worked all morning under the scorching sun of an early summer at the finishing touches and final adjustments to the almost completed work). The lemon trees were already giving off a strong fragrance and, as for him, he was singing in his powerful, musical voice; sometimes he sang softly, in muted tones, as though he were trying to convey to a circle of intimate friends, the kind of people who could understand him, the deep distress of the bandit being taken away to the galleys: "*Farewell, high mountains and rocky peaks! Farewell, nights bathed in the soft light of the moon! I am not struck down by sickness, and yet I am going to die!*"

It was so beautiful, so poignant! Meanwhile, in the lighted windows of that house which reminded one somewhat of a town hall or a college, shadowy figures stood out, silhouettes clear enough to be recognized from the street; they were the silhouettes of the people in the room—a regular congress of ghosts. There were generals, senators, painters—or rather one painter; he took snuff to avoid smoking (his doctors had forbidden him to smoke); he was slowly dying, and his house was dying with him. In former days, when his body was strong and radiant with health, his house was a cheerful sight, with its green shutters and its garden; from the windows which let in the spring sunshine the view stretched all around, over the smiling, fertile hillsides covered with fruit trees; but little by little the great concrete buildings had sprung up; slowly but surely their relentless encirclement tightened around the now joyless house. And now you saw other faces in the streets. The neighbors no longer recognized one another. Sometimes a window would open and against the dark background of the room a figure would appear; but people said they were ancestral ghosts and nothing but a figment of the imagination. Though the district was now unquestionably elegant and so much more lively, Hebdomeros shunned it in favor of the park where the pine trees grew. They were martyred trees, for a strange epidemic was raging among them, these attractive, friendly trees, so healthy and tonic. Each one bore a stairway made of white wood, twined around its trunk like a giant snake; these spiral staircases ended in a kind of platform, a regular torture-collar which choked the unfortunate tree, on which the man known as King Lear to the habitués of the palace amused himself by spying on the birds, hoping to catch them in little-known poses and expressions. He watched out especially for sparrows. Lying down on the platform, as motionless as a log, he no longer looked like a human being. But he did not look like a statue, either. Even when he turned over to take a few minutes' rest, there was nothing in his attitude reminiscent of those figures that lie on stone sarcophagi, be they Etruscan couples or landgraves armed from head to foot. Nor was there anything that reminded one of those old men with flowing beards and gentle eyes, indecently naked and regally reclining among reeds, with their elbows supported by amphorae lying on their sides, and who in ancient statuary represented rivers, the source of the richness of lands.

Nor did he remind one of how gladiators lay, or warriors wounded or dying. This strange man looked more as though he were petrified, which reminded him somewhat of the corpses uncovered at Pompeii. Through lying so long on the platform, he was finally becoming part of it; he was becoming *platformized*; he was turning into something like a large piece of undressed wood, hastily nailed in place to hold up the floor so that it might withstand an impact which would never come. That was why the platform looked upside down as he lay upon it in wait, for a crossbeam meant to strengthen the possible weakness of the planks could only be imagined as being nailed on *underneath*. Seen from such close quarters, the sparrows looked really monstrous. The enigmatic, perturbing, alarming quality of the heads of birds had more than once sent Hebdomeros off into complicated meditation, and he was much given to metaphysical soliloquies in which he thought of quails' heads most of all. Among the other birds' heads which made him uneasy, the hen's took pride of place; the cock's head he found less perturbing, and the goose's and duck's even less so. In general, he considered birds' heads as bad omens, as bearers of misfortune. He thought of the Egyptians, providing their painted or sculptured figures with birds' heads as a homeopathic cure for their fears and superstitious apprehensions: evil driving out evil. And he thought of people in Italy making the sign of horns (the devil) for the same reason when they met with something they were superstitiously afraid of. These thoughts came to him mostly when he was in the garden near the pine grove; lying about among the ill-kept flower beds of this melancholy garden there were bronze hoisting frames and bronze pachyderms. A rhinoceros was standing knee-deep in the farmyard manure heap; and behind the wall, on the other side of this ridiculous partition which merely served to mark off the different areas to prevent quarreling among the neighbors and keep them from trampling on one another's cabbages and lettuces, stood the *inn*. It wasn't, alas, the kind of inn that gave joy and comfort to our grandparents, that cheers and refreshes us, that causes us to dwell on immortality and on the theory that nothing is lost, nothing destroyed, everything living on in other shapes and other forms of matter, the kind of inn that makes us think about the transmigration of souls, just as the Roman countryside does on days when the grape harvest is taken in. The thought of the grape harvest made Hebdomeros think back to those days, which were far from being as simple as they at first appeared.

Across the clear autumn sky sailed great white statuesque clouds, amid which, in poses of sublime majesty, lay the wingless genii; it was at such moments that the explorer would come out onto the balcony of his suburban house, out of his room whose walls were covered with furs and with photographs depicting ships, as black as ink against the whiteness of ice floes; the explorer would muse as he gazed at the great wingless genii lying on the clouds; he would think then of the unfortunate polar bears, desperately clinging to the drifting icebergs, and tears would come to his eyes; he recalled his own journeys, his stopovers in the snow, and the slow, arduous process of sailing in the cold waters of the north. "*Give me your cold seas, I will warm them in mine!*" This was the courtesy that gods alone can show! I say gods, for there are two of them; yes, there are two: White Neptune and Black Neptune, which is the same as saying the god of the North and the god of the South, and it was the black god that had just said these words, stretching out his seaweed-laden arms to his white colleague across the vastness of the world. Hebdomeros deduced from all this that the black race is more polite than any of the others, and also that it has a warmer heart and more sensitive soul; he had even known painters among the Negroes, and one of them had distinguished himself with a painting submitted to the Salon called *Caucasus and Golgotha*. Its meaning was somewhat obscure, but the painting, because of its balanced appearance, had won nevertheless a silver medal; the year before, the same Negro had won an honorable mention for a painting entitled *In Flagrante*. But instead of portraying the drama of adultery, the artist had shown a dog, a griffon terrier, coming unexpectedly upon a pair of sparrows pecking at the cherries set out for the master's breakfast on a table in the garden. The painting *Caucasus and Golgotha* depicted a wide, dusty road bordered by a rather low outcrop of rock which digging and blasting had pitted and furrowed in many places as Cronus does the faces of old men. On this rock stood three crosses around which Roman legionaries were bustling, men with imperial profiles and double chins held in by their helmet straps; there were weeping women, too, and men in breeches carrying ladders; below, on the road, Hebdomeros could be seen sitting on a stone, in the pose of Renan in the famous *Renan in Front of the Parthenon* by André Brouillé. The artist had depicted Hebdomeros in a pensive mood looking at a far-off landscape of factories and smoking chimneys. *An artist's thought is profound*—these were the opening words of an article that the famous critic Étienne Spartali had devoted to the Negro painter in one of the most important newspapers of the capital. And yet, in spite of the articles and studies that were written about it, the work of this painter remained a mystery to everyone. As he was known to be a friend of the painter, Hebdomeros was questioned by several people, but to all he replied that he knew no more about it than anyone else and that, moreover, he would have considered it very indiscreet to question the Negro on the subject; he always liked to observe great tactfulness in his personal relationships; in his opinion, tact was one of the chief human virtues, and he could not have borne for a moment the thought that his friends found him lacking in it.

Apart from all this, the days went by rather monotonously for Hebdomeros. He rose early each morning, almost always wakened by the noise, laughter, and talk of the servants in the house opposite, as the window of his bedroom faced onto a courtyard. In the morning, when he rose and, still half asleep, went to open the shutters of his room, he saw facing him the back of the building which adjoined his; it was always the same scene that met his eyes: maids brushing clothes at the kitchen windows, and just opposite his own window an artillery colonel's orderly would be carefully folding his master's trousers, as he did every day, after wiping them with a cloth soaked in benzine. This soldier was assiduously courting a maid, and both of them looked mockingly at Hebdomeros each time he appeared at the window. The maid, a very blonde girl with quite a good figure, who had been nicknamed "the dragonfly" by one of Hebdomeros's friends, was much friendlier to her neighbor when the colonel's orderly wasn't there. She rather liked Hebdomeros's worried, thoughtful appearance and sometimes when she saw him looking out of the window she asked him if he were homesick; he never gave a very straight answer on these occasions. The young maid's liking for Hebdomeros grew stronger as time went by, and she felt she would have come to love him if an unexpected incident had not suddenly shattered her dearest dreams and illusions. One afternoon, toward the end of a beautiful April day, the servant girl was at the kitchen window, busy cleaning a silver teapot; she was alone, and thinking of Hebdomeros; at that moment she saw him coming out into the courtyard with three of his friends. One of them, having spied in a corner an old shoe with a flapping sole, had the idea of kicking it around with a well-aimed toe; at once Hebdomeros, delighted, put his hat, his cane, and his overcoat on the sill of a first-floor window and he, too, began to chase the old shoe ahead of him with swift kicks; and so the four friends improvised a soccer game using the old shoe; but the wildest and the most excited of all was Hebdomeros, who, having completely lost his homesick look, jumped about like a savage, howling with joy each time the tip of his foot, coming in contact with the old shoe, sent it soaring off among his friends who ducked, shouting, having a wonderful time. Heartsick, the young maid closed the window, placed the half-polished teapot on the kitchen table, and sat down on a stool, disappointed and weary. "And I," she thought sadly, "who believed that he, at least, *was not like the others!*"

Sometimes, on a Sunday morning, before the noise of the servants ended his sleep, a sweet song came to soothe Hebdomeros's last moments of rest; the singing came from a girls' orphanage and each time it plunged him into a black despair; he remembered that in his childhood he had felt the same sadness when in the evening after the sun had set he heard the chirping of the sparrows as they gathered in the trees to pass the night. He thought that his sadness was caused by the fact that the chirping of the sparrows and the singing of the young orphans reproached him for not being *pure enough*; and so, to distract himself, he rambled at length through the countryside; steeple bells in the villages hailed him from the distance; naked children, their bodies skinny, bathed in the clear waters of rushing streams, and near the beaches, under three feet of water, the corpses of pirates moved slowly back and forth, as seaweed moves even when the sea is calm.

The crossing of that lake which was as vast as an ocean, where terrible storms sometimes broke suddenly, dazed Hebdomeros a little, but not enough to make him forget the country house of a general, head of a large, turbulent family. On nights when he could not sleep he lay in his room on the ground floor and stared at the ceiling dimly lit from outdoors; sometimes a shadow passed across it; a shape like a huge drawing compass that was opened and closed, or a hurdle at a track meet as it was overturned by a kick, or the stride of someone walking quickly but carefully. He thought of prowlers, of thieves ready to steal the wrought-iron tables and chairs from the garden, and so he sprang from his bed, and, in his nightshirt and with bare feet, like a matricide being led to the gallows, and grasping his hunting rifle between his hands, he gently edged the door open and peered out: nothing, no one; the vast desert of the night; a moonless summer night, but soft, clear, and solemn; from far off came the echo of the waterfalls rushing down from the tops of those high mountains which men, greedy for marble, had hacked at and torn away in many places; the echo died away in the deep valleys darkened by the shadows of the plane trees. "It must have been a stray dog playing tricks on me," he thought, going back to bed after standing his rifle in a corner. But now it was no longer a *bedroom*, the refuge of a weary traveler; the whole family of the general stood around the oval table and gulped down their meal of rice with peppers, holding their plates up to their chins with their left hands, the way barbers hold their porcelain bowls when they rub alum and water on the freshly shaved cheeks of their customers. The children, who had dinner earlier with their governesses at a separate table, now amused themselves firing their Winchesters at the first bats who zigzagged through the gathering darkness like drunken birds; a few seconds after each report the acrid odor of the smokeless powder floated through the open windows. Moreover, this head of a family, this general, was ruining himself at cards. He would play until dawn in hotels, while the guests lay sleeping, with cardsharps who stripped him of everything he owned; and the next day there would be the humiliation of taking the silverware and the family heirlooms to the pawnshop, and of borrowing money from the servants. Night had not yet fallen completely. In electric trains as brightly lit as theaters, hopes were setting off on a journey, toward that enchanted gulf lit up on one side by the full moon, newly risen, and on the other by the floodlights of the luxurious hotels along the waterfront; there, where only the soft light of the moon held sway, a gentle mist blanketed the outline of the shore; the sky cast a gray-violet shade upon the water where hundreds of small boats, with sheaves of wheat decorating their bows, drifted as in a dream; in each of them a young peasant girl, blonde and very beautiful, in a tight-laced velvet bodice, and with her arms bare, rowed gently and rhythmically; this was paradise, paradise on earth. But the men, except for Hebdomeros, hesitated, for there was merrymaking on the other side: the whirring excitement of the open-air theaters under those acetylene lamps which drew the demented moths to them to be burned. Fat bankers, their faces flushed from alcohol and from overeating, made frightful scenes; they threatened the headwaiters, who were pale with terror, with having them fired, reducing them to poverty, ruining them completely. When it was the hour to return, to go back to those luxurious waiting villas, built among the ruins, where the lizards, immortal because they were ever renascent, slithered over the ancient stones like lightning, as they did in the days when the blossoming arbors and the artificial grottoes rang with the call of that squint-eyed man, the regional, who never knew what to do with his hands or where to put that fatal cane which had been lost and found again in the canals of red-hued Venice—"*Svetonia! Svetonia!*"— but it was only the memory of an echo. The wives were waiting for them; they had a never-failing patience, for often the roistering continued until the early dawn, and then there were endless pleas that they spare their husbands; they offered to go and work on their lands; to be yoked to the plow like animals, to toil anywhere, asking nothing in return; to harvest the hemp in the midsummer heat, sunk to their knees in the mud of the marshes, devoured by the mosquitoes with proboscises thirsty for blood. These tearful prayers often went on until dawn;

until that moment when the blazing sun rose in triumphant splendor behind those nearby low-lying mountains, setting fire to the gold on the pediments of the miniature temples that were like huge toys and chastely tinting with pink the statues which stood on low pedestals. Everything came to life, and the black demons, dulled by lack of sleep and by indigestion, were chased back to their dismal palaces, while the joyful song of the blacksmiths and the noise of the rustic carts, crammed with carrots and turnips, lurching heavily along the hard, cobbled roads, was heard. To defend the town, to oppose, with a handful of timorous invalids, the fierce invaders who had landed from ships which covered them with long-range guns, and who were even now advancing, arms at the ready, would have been sheer madness. Courageous though he was, Hebdomeros could understand the futility of such a gesture; he led his companions to a safe place, and, having left them sufficient provisions, he headed toward a damp, wooded mountain, where he might recover his strength and his lost hopes.

In the parks which smelled of plants rotted by the extreme dampness, the clearings were haunted, during the rare days of fine weather, by the presence of a man of genius, a Cabinet Minister, whose servants, as faithful as they were well-trained, rolled his wheelchair there; this distinguished invalid suffered from a highly pernicious disease which made it necessary that he always lie in his chair at a certain angle, so that he should not take a turn for the worse and die suddenly from the stagnant urine in his system, for he could only urinate with great difficulty (and sometimes went for days without doing so at all). Stretched out in his wheelchair, his legs wrapped in rugs and shawls to his knees, he lay there, under the taciturn watch of his servants, until sunset, his expression vacant, his mind a blank. Another ghost, a multilingual old man, on those nights when the moon was full, moved by the impressive sight of the slumbering trees with their leaves shivering in the shadows, persisted in posing invariably the same questions: "*Where is it all going?* Toward what unknown shores do all these things sail? . . ." And then, in order to break the mood—the *Stimmung*, as Hebdomeros called it—created by such questions, some cynical, athletic young men responded by imitating with their mouths the sound of a long and sonorous fart. And then there was the rain; rain today like yesterday and like tomorrow; a steady rain, if not a heavy one; an endless rain; all the trees took the shape of weeping willows.

Shepherds in rags, soaked to their skins, stood leaning on their long crooks, surrounded by their melancholy flocks. Hebdomeros felt that the dampness was getting the better of him, too; he was cold in his bed for the sheets were never really dry; he found moss growing in the closets where he hung his clothes, as it does in a cave; gloomy toads jumped sluggishly about in the little garden of the hotel where he lodged.

Once again he had to leave, to quit those parts. Hebdomeros asked to pay his bill and said goodbye to the hotelkeeper, who did his best to show him that the rain wouldn't last forever and that the year before, at the same season, the weather had been magnificent; besides, the barometer was rising; some of the old people insisted that the birds were chirping in that special way which indicated a change in the direction of the wind; it would begin to blow from the north and that would clear the sky: "You know, Mr. Hebdomeros," the hotelkeeper added, twisting the buttons on his client's overcoat familiarly and brushing off his shoulders, "you know, in clear weather we have a wonderful view from here; first, in the distance, on the plain, you see the town with the cathedral, the towers of the old town hall, the river which flows through the middle of the town, and the bridges, which are real works of art; then, around it, the whole ring of hills, and their villas with flowered terraces. With my sailor's telescope you can even catch a glimpse of people leaning out the windows; then further to the west are the famous peaks known as the Dragon's Teeth; they are always covered with snow, and more than one reckless mountain climber has fallen from their precipices to his death. And there, to the north, you see the sea with the port and the mass of factories and workshops which are always busy, and which have made our region famous for their industriousness." Hebdomeros listened to him politely; he would have liked to tell him that he hated panoramas, that he liked nothing but rooms, good rooms where one could shut oneself up, with the curtains drawn and the doors closed; and especially the corners of rooms and low ceilings; but he didn't say a word about all the things he preferred, afraid he wouldn't be understood, and even more afraid that people would think him mad and report him to the local medical authorities. So he paid his hotel bill, which was rather high for the place and the time of year, and went off down toward the plain. The town was surrounded by high volcanic mountains and the heat was stifling; a young engineer who worked on building an extension of the railroad line exclaimed over and over that he had had enough of life, that he was sick of it. When he went into the little restaurant where he always ate, he would go to the kitchen before he sat down at a table to peep into the pots and see what had been cooked; he was on very good terms with the chef, to whom, from time to time, he made gifts of obscene photographs; in return the chef described his erotic prowess, most of which was imaginary. The town was full of hot fountains, some of them sulfurous. The hotel Hebdomeros stayed at was some distance from the sea; nevertheless, a bronze sea-god, armed with a trident and mounted on a dolphin, stood guard over the main entrance. Hebdomeros felt the attachment which bound him to this hotel; he felt how this bond grew each day; he thought of the hour of separation, and that thought caused him deep sadness; but he could do nothing else; no other solution came to him; it had to be done, "It must be done, my dear, it's an atonement," as the captain said, to appease his conscience, gallantly offering his arm to his wife; both were in excellent spirits that day, for they knew they had been invited to dine in the evening with the colonel commanding the garrison and that the dinner would be followed by a glittering reception. The hour of his leaving sounded. A servant who might have been a model for Giotto had to haul Hebdomeros off like a rag to a second-class carriage of the local that left at two o'clock. Then came the endless journey, the long and inexplicable halts at small, deserted stations lost in the middle of the countryside. Butchers' boys slept, face down, their heads covered with their bloodstained aprons to keep off the flies that attacked them ferociously, as if they were carcasses; and the cicadas chirped obsessively in the dust-colored fig trees that were petrified by the heat. Chieftains, barbarian kings, as motionless as statues on their small white horses harnessed in carnival fashion like the steeds of Saracen leaders, their heads held high and their right hands proudly planted on their armor-clad thighs, watched the long line of the invading hordes moving to the west, driving before them the cattle stolen from the peasants. Now and then a soldier with parched throat would search the dried-up riverbeds for a last drop of water; and when fate was kind he crouched like a panther to slake his thirst eagerly; and then he filled his helmet with water and holding it with great care, like the novice maidservant carrying a soup tureen, he climbed from the gully to rejoin his fellows; for all these fierce and fatalistic warriors were at heart both kind and generous; they thought always of the friend, the companion, the sick leader wracked by swamp fever, who lay sweating on the straw in a wagon. Often the prisoners of this invincible horde were amazed to see that the leaders, whose rank would have entitled them to every attention, were treated when wounded or sick like the humblest, most obscure soldier; but they themselves wished this; and it was this, too, which explained the strength of that horde which no enemy could withstand. There was nothing to show which of the wagons used to transport the sick and wounded the chiefs lay in. Only Hebdomeros held himself aloof from these great migrations. He stared at the outline of the sands, which even now the desert winds whirled into inverted cones, their points touching the ground, rising like smoke into the threatening sky, curling into the biblical shapes of Jewish candelabra, lit now and then by a flash of lightning which appeared between them like tripods hurled from the sky, like that mysterious geometric angel, that angel as stripped as a tree in autumn, that angel unadorned and dry, that angel which had nothing but the indispensable, the strictly necessary, and which Hebdomeros saw one day leaping from one floor of a large apartment house to another and swoop into a room, near a bed where, surrounded by his officers, dismay written on their faces, and by his weeping family, an aged general lay dying. Having received the soul of the dead, the angel again assumed the aspect of a tripod launched into space and carried the soul to heaven. In the eternal realms the soul of the general took the form of the purest smoke. The sea of stars stretched into the distance, as if the sky no longer seemed to be a dome but a ceiling instead. Captive balloons, their shapes ridiculous and obscene, floated aimlessly above the parade ground as Hebdomeros went into a huge tavern packed with people who were drinking and where the smoke from pipes and cigars was so thick that one had to make headway bellowing, as steamboats do on days of heavy fog. Hebdomeros claimed that an elderly barmaid in that tavern was in love with him. "In her love," he said, speaking to one of his young friends, "there is something of a mother's love." But the real reason he went to the tavern was his hope of meeting a shaggy-haired, ruddy-faced man, wearing horn-rimmed glasses, and whose shirts were never quite clean, but who, among both the staff and the customers, had the reputation of unfailing kindness. He had been seen to weep; he was writing his memoirs, and when at dawn he left his suburban house, built at the edge of a forest which was partially depleted but still impressive, he sometimes lingered a long time, his hand resting on the bolt of the garden gate, to look with nostalgia and deep feeling at the facade of that house, modest although stylized and baroque, which he had inherited from his father and where his sons, with their wives and children, would doubtless continue to live. Sometimes, at moments like this, the moon in its final quarter spread its dim glow over the house, giving it a sweet sadness. He also had the reputation of being a kind of antidote for bad luck and the evil eye; malevolent visions, monks pursuing sows and their piglets, or very tall women with the heads of birds would vanish at his approach. But his outstanding quality was the exquisite, infinite sensitivity of his soul. Must we therefore conclude that he was a sentimentalist and a dreamer? One of those whom life tosses about like flotsam on a stormy sea? Alas, no! *Wir zahlen Geld*; *we pay cash*; these were the first words of the classified ad he had placed in the papers. Attracted by this tempting offer, Hebdomeros set off through dark streets filled with silent crowds; he climbed squalid stairways flanked by leprous walls and covered with obscene graffiti, and at last he encountered this man, this apostle whom he had imagined more than once in his childhood dreams as someone roaming around the world with a pack on his back and a pilgrim's staff in his hand, his head held high, his eyes shining, like all those who trek far across the desolate plains toward the white cities, knowing that their brothers are waiting there, under the porticos, watching for them eagerly; so when Hebdomeros found himself in the presence of this man, whom his father had sheltered for more than a month so that he could look after his shinbone which had been bruised by the flying hooves of a mule, this man who, when Hebdomeros was a child, had more than once taken him to the theater and had shown him, on provincial stages, the Devil firing a rifle in a room, then opening the window and leaping into space like a diver into water, Hebdomeros saw a sneering, myopic man who burst out laughing at the sight of him; in almost no time all the inkwells had been knocked over, so much did he shake the tables in pounding them with his fists between guffaws. "*Pay money! Pay money!*" he yelled, bubbling over with laughter, roaring as if he were possessed. "But, my good man, what about your real estate? Yes, where is your real estate? And your stocks? And your bonds?" The scales suddenly fell from Hebdomeros's eyes. A feeling of terrible shame swept over him in a great shudder and his face turned scarlet. He wanted only to flee, to flee, yes, to flee; no matter where, no matter how, simply to flee; to leave this place, to disappear. He would perhaps go to China; he would live the life of a night owl in the pagodas that shone like huge lanterns, and then at noon, in a hammock hung between two blossoming cherry trees, he would take a siesta; he would fall asleep in the midday warmth, and the goats, reassured by his immobility, would warily approach and begin to nibble gently at the leaves of the creepers nearby.

But now, unable to turn back that inexorable flow of immigration toward the west, Hebdomeros found himself again in the same town, or rather it seemed the same, although something had changed in the layout of the streets and the location of the castle; boats or, more precisely, punts were moored at the banks of the river, where the water, reflecting the sky covered with clouds at twilight, had a whitish, milky color which contrasted sharply with the dark and almost black tint of the bank; the punts, too, were silhouetted as dark forms against the limpid water; this gave them the vague appearance of funeral gondolas, and suggested the tragedy of Venice during the epidemics of the plague and the deaths of the great painters who were struck down by the relentless scourge. Meanwhile the sky grew darker and darker until, at last, night had spread its somber wings over the whole region. Hebdomeros passed behind a cattle shed, where the window, on his side, was at the level of a man's head, for the back of the building faced a street higher than that where the front door was. He went up to the window and looked through it. Although the light from the lanterns the peasants had hung in the corners was dim, he still could clearly see the large prehistoric stone fonts where, according to legend, lay the remains of the first five fabulous kings who governed the town; later they had been used by washerwomen for scrubbing clothes; and now the peasants put their cows in them when they were about to calve; and there, in that large stone cistern devoid of all decoration (this by no means spoiled its appearance), Hebdomeros saw *him* and saw himself, naked and kneeling, like Isaac offering himself up for sacrifice:

Oh, gentle lamb of Isaac to the altar attached,
Don't count your chickens before they're hatched.

Silent, stern-faced men, their sleeves rolled up on their Herculean arms, bent over him, carefully shearing him; one could make out the flash of the steel blades in the semidarkness of the cow shed. At the right, a ray of moonlight coming through a small window of the roof splashed light, like silver and mercury, into a corner; opposite, a lantern on the ground shone on a cow lying on manure with her little calf; a young peasant girl dozed on a bench near the group of animals, her back against the wall, her head fallen on her breast, and her arms around a child lying on her lap; Hebdomeros, observing the two scenes of the cow and the peasant girl, thought that if a painter had depicted them in a picture he would have called his canvas *The Two Mothers*; and at the same time Hebdomeros thought of the death of the Duke of Enghien; it was the shadows cast on the wall by the lantern on the ground that awakened naturally these memories in a man with a vivid imagination and a head stuffed with ideas acquired from reading. And yet, at the bottom of the fonts, they were singing as only the love-stricken nightingale can sing deep in a flowered garden on a sweet summer night. Hebdomeros would have lingered much longer at the window of the shed to watch the strange scenes taking place inside, if he had not been hailed point-blank by one whom all the town called *the madman* because, without being a gourmet, he was interested only in questions of eating. Whenever he met a friend or even an acquaintance, in the street or elsewhere, he never failed to stop him, no matter where or when the meeting took place, and there and then he would question him remorselessly to learn what he had eaten for lunch or dinner. Furthermore, wherever he went he carried a thin metal stick with a sharp point; often, as he returned home late at night, he rummaged in the garbage cans that stood before the carriage gates of houses. He often said, to anyone willing to listen, that he loved sausage and rice. However, as Hebdomeros understood it, the unrestrained, lunatic way of life of this peculiar gourmet did not last much longer. The season of his important meteorological work approached; it was already the end of March, and in early April he would have to seclude himself up there, in the turret of his castle. That was the period when, cut off from the world, he refused to see anyone; should canvassers, journalists, or simply the bothersome or the curious ring his bell, the maid, after having asked the ritual question: *What name shall I give?* answered invariably: *The gentleman has gone out*, or: *The gentleman is not in*, or else: *The gentleman has gone out on an errand*; to this last answer obstinate visitors replied that they would wait until *the gentleman* had returned from his errand;—*Oh, no*, the maid then added, unabashed, *that is quite impossible, for when the gentleman goes out on an errand he stays away for several days* ... Besides, he not only closed his door to everyone but he also refused to go home at mealtime. Immersed in a comparative study of his improved wind gauges, he forgot, in the midst of an indescribable disorder, life with all its train of worries, of pains, of pleasures, and of joys. From time to time his wife and daughter, real models of devotion, took advantage of the rare moments when he was overcome by fatigue and lack of food and fell asleep for a short time; then they crept into his small office on tiptoe and, after having left a tray with a roll, pancakes, salted cheese, some dates, and a decanter of cold coffee on the table, they withdrew walking backward without taking their eyes off him, for woe to them if he caught them in his room! One felt this was a life which could not continue. Emma, the daughter, had hysterics every evening. The father sought to wheedle his son, Marius, who was a cook in Marseilles, by offering him cigarettes, and so the night wore on and toward the first glimmer of dawn an officer without a tunic, his shirt open on his chest, passed, weaving between the haystacks; he rode a horse without a saddle, both legs on the same side, as women ride; blood flowed from a long gash on his left cheek and stained his shirt; he seemed not to notice it; at first he had refused the duel: "Fight?" he exclaimed in a surprised tone. "Fight in front of a woman?"; with a quick gesture he pointed out the young girl in a flowered bodice who remained seated in the middle of the meadow in the pose of a Joan of Arc who hears *the voices*; nevertheless, he had been forced to fight and that which had to happen happened ... Now the hours had passed, slowly, inevitably, as all hours pass. The sun was high in a sky without clouds, but which was veiled slightly by a fine haze that heralded summer; not a breath of wind; the strong smell of wine, raw and rotting, rose from the deep caves where monks and smugglers, hounded out by the new government, snored, dead drunk and lying jumbled one on top of another. The shadow on the sundial marked noon; however, some moments later the state of the atmosphere changed; oh! it wasn't one of those brusque changes such as occur in America and in certain regions of equatorial Africa where, all at once, while the sky is pure and the air still, black clouds charged with electricity invade the celestial vault, plunging the country into apocalyptic darkness, while tremendous squalls of rain and wind overturn all in their paths, whirling stable doors and the wooden benches of parks as high as housetops; no, happily these cataclysms, as deadly as unexpected, were far distant; the change which had taken place in the atmosphere was so little perceptible that any man less observant and sensitive than Hebdomeros would never have noticed it; but indeed the air was no longer still; the weather vane on the steeple, which represented a stylized rooster, turned slightly. Hebdomeros, who detested the atmosphere of the *end of spring*, that languorous closeness which relentlessly heralds the hot months, the approach of that season which a great poet termed *violent*, understood that the wind from the sea was coming at last and he rejoiced with all his heart; he also had a foreboding that he was to take part in some inexplicable phenomena which would force him to long and profound meditation; the cool and gentle wind, the wind of hope and solace, persisted. Until then all had gone well, but suddenly the cock, or rather that silhouette, that projected shadow of a cock, became more and more obsessing and began to dominate the landscape and to play a role in the life of this humble and peaceful corner; it was a place and a role that would never have been previously suspected; now it actually *descended*; at the same time it *rose*; acting like a corrosive, on one side it *ate* the steeple while, on the other, standing out against it and spreading out with a slow and inexplicable regularity, it sliced into the sky. Now the feet of the cock touched the ground and his comb the clouds; white letters, solemn letters like those carved in stone, advanced a little from all directions, hesitated, sketched in the air a kind of out-of-date quadrille, and finally decided to pair up at the wish of a mysterious force and formed this strange inscription at some distance from the ground:

SCIO DETARNAGOL BARA LETZTAFRA

Suddenly the whole *outdoors* lost its atmosphere, its *Stimmung*; a violent light *from the side* lit the rafters and the floorboards. "It's a trick of the local photographer," people whispered in cafés and in the local squares. Again a movement; a stage set is changed, a screen drawn aside, a curtain raised and here is *the dance*; the celebration in the American *megaron*; luxury and lewdness display their fireworks, their evil beacons in the vast halls, decorated with a lavishness and a cleverness completely unknown before; the guests, whose quadruple-plated safes are stuffed with bank notes, give themselves up to a frantic orgy; they swim in it with the movements of divers turning about under the water; through the great windows open on the night the sky with all its constellations multiplying to infinity is seen; the city and its austere temples, all white on the sacred rocks, is seen, too, and the she-wolf, hideously gilded, suffering the torture of the ravenous twins clinging to her long teats. Hebdomeros just had time to jump into a dark corner from which he could watch all these strange scenes at his ease, and without being seen. "*May the universe crumble*," cried the voice of a monarch from somewhere down there, by the terraces whose walls and arches were hugged by climbing plants. A gallop of horses, the heavy rhythmic footsteps of a cohort marching toward the northern gate; *porta collina profectus est*; swollen by the recent rains, the torrents roared and foamed under the bridges; and now the scene changes again; the wind chases the clouds and then there is a desperate flight of the moon behind them; sometimes the moon disappears for a while and all at once it seems that the whole earth has been muffled like a wooden bell; then its rays pass through the clouds again as the wind blows them apart; the silent phalanxes of gladiators march all around. Hebdomeros was gazing at that woman and child when, suddenly, the immense iron gates of the garden were sent crashing as if at the passage of a hurricane, and the *barbarians* appeared at the door of the salon, standing in their stirrups, hurling their cry of war and making their long whips with leaded thongs crack horribly, sweeping everything before them; … the voice that sang ceased …; the director of an important shipping company, who lived on the second floor of a comfortable house, turned toward the wall in his sleep; the springs creaked and, while still sleeping, he grumbled something incomprehensible: but in the movement that he made he uncovered his left arm up to his elbow and Hebdomeros, who had for an hour been patiently awaiting his awakening, saw that on his arm he had a most curious tattoo; a vintage model of a locomotive encircled by a serpent swallowing his own tail was portrayed. Another peculiarity of the director was that he always kept a large life belt placed on the floor and leaning against the foot of the bed.—"It's best to be prepared," he would reply to people who questioned him about this strange habit, "for you never know what might happen." His wife, however, could never get used to seeing that life belt placed at the foot of the bed; she found it rather funereal; not without reason she thought of it as a morbid idea, and she also saw it as a bad omen, a herald of misfortune. "You will see, Martiobarbulus," she said to her husband, "you'll see that this life belt is so like a funeral wreath that sooner or later it will finish by bringing you misfortune." But just try to persuade one so obstinate. Hebdomeros had to flee. He went all around his room in a boat, continually forced into a corner by the undercurrent and, at last, abandoning his frail craft and gathering all his strength and skill as a former gymnast, he hoisted himself up to the window which was placed very high, like the window of a prison, helping himself by the moldings. Then his heart beat with joy, and with what joy! From there he took in at a glance the whole vast, comforting panorama of those palaestrae mosaicked with white rectangles, squares, and trapezoids where young athletes were throwing their discus with classical movements, or running races, heads thrust into their shoulders and flung behind, like stags hunted down by hounds. When in the afternoon after a frugal meal eaten in the company of champion jumpers and champion boxers, perfect gentlemen all, who while they excused themselves for their lack of luxury and their simple fare insisted each time on paying for his meal, he made his way to that city built like a fortress, having interior courtyards and oblong, geometric gardens which relieved the severe shape of the ramparts, he always found the same well-built men there, perfectly healthy in body and mind, and engaged in their favorite occupation: the making of trophies. And thus strange scaffoldings loomed in the middle of bedrooms and salons, austere but at the same time droll; joy and amusement for guests and children. Constructions which took the form of mountains, for like mountains they had been born of an inner fire, and once they had passed through the upheaval of creation, their contorted yet balanced forms bore witness to the burst of fire that had brought them into being; by this very fact they were *pyrophiles*; which is to say that, like salamanders, they *loved fire*; they were immortal for they knew neither dawn nor dusk, only eternal noon. The rooms which sheltered them were like those islands which are found outside the main sea routes and where the inhabitants sometimes wait entire seasons until a tanker or a friendly sailing ship comes to throw them a few cases of spoiled preserves; like these islands they were outside the human mainstream; outside, without at the same time being so remote as not to notice the passage and not to hear the echoes of those armies on the march, of those unending lines of honest workers crossing again and again the bridges slung from steel pylons, first in the morning in the half-light of dawn to get to their screeching, sweltering factories, and then in the evening to return to their peaceful homes and humbly share bread and meat with their wives and their children. And if sometimes Hebdomeros let himself be too trusting, that signified neither that he was an innocent nor a fanatic; he wanted to *believe*: he forced himself to believe that such and such a man was intelligent; and then he solemnly stated so among his friends and acquaintances and tried to dupe himself; and yet he knew that in reality *it was not exactly like that*; among those with the anxious irritated expressions, among those impotent and annoyed intellectuals who feared and hated irony and true talent and haunted certain cafés where they arrived carrying under their arms, like a relic, the latest volume of their favorite poet, who was inevitably and like them impotent, sterile, and constipated, and in whom they recognized themselves perfectly, but whom a benign fate and a combination of circumstances had brought into prominence, giving him the sweet illusion of fame, those who then placed on the table next to their coffee with cream the adored volume, printed in a few numbered copies, of which the middle of each page of Japanese vellum was disfigured by two or three short lines of pseudoesoteric foolishness and pretentious twaddle, in all those whom he recognized at once by certain exterior signs which never failed him, in all these manufacturers of superfluous art and literature, men with suspicious expressions, whose mouths had never laughed with candor, Hebdomeros sensed a *binding*; he sensed that a *knot* prevented them from moving their arms and legs freely, from running, climbing, jumping, swimming, and diving, from recounting something with wit, from writing and painting—in a word, from *comprehending*. And often, in many, even among those who in the throng of their fellows enjoyed a reputation for intelligence, he saw the knot and the powerlessness to comprehend; because of this the knot was for Hebdomeros a sign infinitely more profound and disturbing than the ithyphallic sign or that of the anchor or the two-edged axe. The *knot-people*, as he called them, were for Hebdomeros the living and walking symbol of human stupidity. Moreover, he saw life as a huge knot which death untied; and yet he also regarded death as a knot retied which birth in turn undid; sleep was for him the *double knot*; the complete untying of the knot lay according to him in eternity, beyond birth and death. However, these obscure workings of fate did not prevent men from going about their business. Monday and Friday were market days; on those days agents and traders made their way to the town from all inhabited corners of this flat and monotonous region in long, silent files and gathered in the marketplace. Many of them were people

suffering from venereal diseases become chronic because of early neglect; they took advantage of their brief
stay in the city to consult specialists in the afternoon;
the latter never failed, whatever their clients' trouble, to
give them appointments for the following week. Toward
the end of the day the square slowly emptied; in long
black files the syphilitic and gonorrheal traders returned
to the neighboring towns, and the square became deserted as if troops had swept it with repeated salvos of
rifle fire. The only trace of the departed crowd was rubbish of all kinds strewn on the paving stones; but what
predominated was orange peel and crushed cigar stubs;
over this distressing scene bronze warriors maintained
their bellicose gestures, as if followed by phalanxes of
fanatical soldiers who were visible to them alone, and
the sages in stone, the marble politicians, sometimes
sullied by city smoke, the bald, unknown great men
leaned over their books, their instruments, and their
scrolls. The sun sank low on the horizon, spreading its
rays along the main municipal road, that road which
linked the city with its neighboring towns. Shepherds
who at that hour were following this road to return to
their hamlets toward the west received full in the eyes
all this late wealth of light; it prevented them from seeing their flocks and annoyed them intensely. They flew
into a rage and swore at their dogs, which, panic-stricken
by their masters' reproaches, began running and barking right and left and being more nuisance than help; in
order to see better, the shepherds, still muttering oaths,

put their left hands to their foreheads like visors while with the right they brandished the long crooks they were never without and which, seen in profile, resembled the helmets of warriors painted on Grecian vases. The sun's rays lengthened now almost horizontally over the crimson dust of the road, and the shadows of shepherds and crooks also lengthened; they lengthened beyond measure, monstrously, they crossed towns, countries, and seas, they reached the far-off land of the Cimmerians, there where frozen winds secure the snow a long time on the mountains; they touched those lands whose inhabitants are dressed all year round in thick furs and have a complicated and obscene mythology.

And then the sun disappeared completely behind the line of low hills at the horizon; the shadows climbed into the sky and stretched themselves out over the earth, while up there on the left, in the now-clear sky, the crescent of the moon shone hard and cold, and the purifying breezes of the approaching night blew over the town where the last echoes of the labor of men were dying away.

Having left the town, Hebdomeros stopped in a valley which lay a short distance away from the highest mountain rising in the east. At any moment he was to begin a long nocturnal climb and needed to gather his strength, so he sat down on a stone where he had first placed his carefully folded coat and plunged into deep thought; slowly, with each memory from the past, the curtain rose. Hebdomeros abandoned himself happily to this nostalgia; it was one of his principal weaknesses always to have a certain nostalgia for the past, even for a past that had been completely fulfilled; that was why he liked also to sleep in the afternoon; he maintained that nothing evokes memories of the past so profoundly as the moments before or immediately following the afternoon nap. To his friends he said that it is simply a question of training, but his friends were not always the intellectually elite he might have desired; they were vigorous young people, and willing, but clumsy and often very slow to grasp and understand the requirements of his exceptional nature and the subtleties of his outstanding mind. "At the beginning," said Hebdomeros in his discourses, "we flounder about and get dirty as we work, we spatter the walls around us; we stain the objects we touch, we get our things into a mess, crumpled papers and grimy rags bestrew the floor; without meaning to we paint ourselves with a clown's face; we go out into the street not knowing that we have arabesques drawn on our back and our nose painted green, which naturally makes people laugh and turn around as we pass by. Then gradually with age and experience, discipline, knowledge, and skill prevail over instinct; we begin to have the air of topflight surgeons, we become at once subtle and forceful; a certain slow deliberation can be seen in everything we do, particularly if one thinks of the ardor of youth; but behind the slowness, in batches, in series, creations pile up one on top of the other, they form an impressive capital, unheard-of reserves; we build supports of a solidity to withstand all tests; we grant unlimited credit to those furnishing the requisite guarantees; we circulate throughout the wide world our fundamental creations; we even send them far away to those still little explored lands which our millenary civilization has as yet but faintly marked with its seal and trademarks; this is why I say to you, my friends: be methodical, don't waste your strength; when you have found a sign, turn it around and around, look at it from the front and from the side, take a three-quarter view and a foreshortened view; remove it and note what form the memory of its appearance takes in its place; observe from which angle it looks like a horse, and from which like the molding on your ceiling; see when it suggests the aspect of a ladder, or a plumed helmet; in which position it resembles Africa, which itself resembles a large heart: the heart of the earth, a vast, heated heart; I dare even say overheated; it beats too fast and needs to adjust itself. According to the predictions of a great poet who died about twenty years ago, it is the continent where the world will know its last great civilization before growing cold forever and sharing the fate of the moon. But for the moment these gloomy predictions don't worry anybody, particularly as you all have long been involved in the difficult game of reversing time and revolving your angle of vision; this may be said without flattering you, for you have always pitted your obstinacy as metaphysical seekers and the tolerant and generous nobility of your elect souls, the souls of born poets, against the mockery of skeptics. And you, who at heart believe even less in space than in time, you have always had faith in the rhythmical march which carries forward the great human races, a march which nothing can resist; you have always lived in the comforting half-light given to your cool rooms by the shutters closed against the ardor of the noonday sun, and in meditation on theorems learned by heart and never to be forgotten, like the evening prayer taught by the bigoted tutor to the wanton child." Thus spoke Hebdomeros, and his disciples, who had been joined by several sailors and some local fishermen, listened to him in silence; but they were pressed more and more closely around him and he was obliged finally to do as Christ did in the same circumstances on the advice of an apostle: he climbed onto a boat moored by the shore and, standing on the prow, continued his inspired discourse. Far off, behind the hills overlooking the town to the east, the first paleness of the dawn was creeping chastely into the sky.

"*What is that murmur which rises from the dark streets?*" asked Lyphontius, the philosopher, lifting his head toward the window of the room where he was working at a table covered with books and papers. He lived in a modest apartment above the porticos which framed the main square of the town. From his window he could see the back of the statue of his father which stood on a low pedestal in the middle of the square. His father also had been a philosopher, and the eminence of his work had moved his fellow citizens to erect this monument in his honor in the middle of the largest and most beautiful square in town. The houses which surrounded this square were fairly low, so that the hills dotted with villas and fine terraced gardens could easily be seen. On the crest of the highest of these hills was a huge structure which was said to be a monastery, but which looked more like a fortress, or even a large barracks or a vast gunpowder depot; it was surrounded by a crenellated wall with arrow slits.

When the black sails of pirate ships appeared far off on the sea, the inhabitants of the villas would run to take refuge in this structure; they took with them their most precious objects, their books, their tools, linen and clothes; no weapons; they abhorred weapons and moreover knew nothing of how to handle them. Not only had they no weapons in their homes but they avoided pronouncing the name of a weapon, particularly in front of their children; the words *revolver*, *pistol*, *rifle*, *dagger* were considered taboo words by these hysterical puritans, and if some stranger, ignorant of these customs, began to talk about weapons, he threw a chill upon the company and created an uneasiness difficult to dispel. If the children happened to be present, the atmosphere became intolerable. The only weapon whose name might be pronounced was the cannon, because people are not in the habit of keeping cannons in their houses. They left nothing in the abandoned villas but a few pieces of old furniture and stuffed animals whose presence in the middle of the empty rooms frightened the first pirates who opened the doors, drunk with massacre and looting.

The refugees in the huge building were, furthermore, extremely comfortable. Plentiful provisions were stacked in the vaults. In the middle of the vast inner courtyards were artistically laid-out gardens, sunny corners where fruit trees grew, flowery arbors, fountains ornamented with fine statues, and even pools where fish swam and where swans of immaculate whiteness glided with their breasts to the wind. All this enabled the refugees to forget their unhappy situation as the besieged and to imagine themselves in one of those spas, true earthly paradises of our planet where city dwellers, fatigued by the continual turmoil of business and the worry of succeeding, go during the torrid summers to nurse their swollen livers and tired stomachs. Hebdomeros could not share the opinion of those skeptics who considered that all this was make-believe and that centaurs had never existed, any more than fauns, sirens, and tritons. As if to prove the contrary, they were all at the door, pawing the ground and chasing with great swishes of their tails the flies which clung obstinately to their twitching flanks; they were all there, those centaurs with their mottled rumps; there were veterans among them; old centaurs larger than the others, although thinner; they looked desiccated and as if under the weight of years their bones had broadened and lengthened; in the shadow of the thick white eyebrows which contrasted curiously with their dark complexions, their eyes were gentle and sky blue like the eyes of Nordic children; their glance was full of an infinite sadness (the sadness of demigods);

it was as attentive and steady as the gaze of sailors or mountain dwellers, or hunters of eagles and chamois, the gaze in general of those accustomed to scanning great distances and distinguishing men, animals, and objects from very far away. The others, more youthful, were landing one another hearty, open-handed slaps and amused themselves by lashing out with their hooves against the fences of the vegetable gardens. Occasionally an adult centaur detached himself from the group and trotted off along the paths going down to the river; there he stopped to chat with the washerwomen who were beating their linen, kneeling on the bank. The younger ones became nervous at the approach of the man-horse. Hebdomeros, who had more than once witnessed the scene, was always intrigued by the anxiety of the young washerwomen, but this time he thought he had discovered the reason for it:—surely it was reminiscences of a mythological nature which troubled them, he told himself, and then followed up his thought:— haunted by these memories, their feminine imagination, always verging on the dramatic, already saw themselves being *carried off*; the centaur crossing the river among the eddies, dragging with him the woman, screaming and disheveled like a drunken bacchante; Hercules on the bank, straining at the bow, panting with exertion as he shoots his poisoned darts; and then the blood-soaked mantle; the mantle whose color deepens to that of the dregs of wine, and which clings like a second skin to the centaur's torso.

But the older washerwomen reassured them, saying there was nothing to fear, at least for the moment; they added after a pause during which they seemed to pursue a memory that it was like the time of the procession: "We dined early that day, a moment or two before sunset, so that when the younger girls cleared away the food left on the table after the meal and shook out the tablecloths stained with gravy and red wine in the yard, the setting sun still illuminated the countryside all around, and lit fires in the windows of the low houses. The procession was climbing up from the low point of that road that dips at one point into the valley, such that to the people watching from the village it looked like a dusty pier extending into a vast sea; the noise of the bells and fireworks was deafening. The column advanced enthusiastically, with banners to the wind, and hoisted aloft like the antennas of ships on stormy seas were strange signs painted and engraved with many a disturbing cipher, departure point of a whole long series of inspirations as capricious as they were surprising, and which were sure guarantees for the tranquil period later, when the voices of the oracles had fallen silent as if the spirit had emigrated far from the earth. Those were the days, my young friends, when it was utterly useless to let oneself be shut up in deserted temples at nightfall by distracted guardians, hoping that sleeping next to the effigy of a divinity would provide the answer to the question marks and open the doors onto the unknown, or even lift the curtains veiling the mystery of the long-closed chambers. Oh ruins! Temples of

Neptune flooded by the sea! Waves buffeting the playful dolphins toward the sanctuary which in normal times even the initiate cannot help but enter with trembling, carrying his muddy sandals in his hand." And now, here at the crossroads, the confusion of the holiday crowds became alarming. Sweating innkeepers rushed to put their tables out on the pavement. People, all wearing some sort of mask, leaned over the low balconies and stared unabashed at the straitlaced passersby. Gods for the day with inscrutable faces and dignified clothes sat at café terraces; everywhere ground-floor rooms with all the windows open and all the lamps lit; an indiscretion, a cynicism, a total abandon truly unheard of; suddenly and without warning locomotives pulling whole trains entered the streets where the crowds were milling about; one couldn't tell where they might have gone, but on reaching the end of the street they took a sharp turn to the left with the classic movement of a goldfish in a bowl and, setting off on the right path, disappeared into the shadows of the countryside; dogs barked in the distance; joyous groups of young people wearing beribboned three-cornered hats passed like whirlwinds, shouting coarse jokes. And in the cafés turned into cubes of smoke the continual tension, the crazy effort to smile at unconscionably stupid jokes, and the silly puns that bounced from one habitué to another: *Que fera le villageois? Que fera le vil?* (question). *Ah! Joie!* (exclamation). Let the cat (imperative) retrace my steps (imperative). And that customer who declared that all the calves in the district were chipping in to buy a wreath for the butcher who had died the previous day.

Might we go back now? The five horses drawing the carriage would set off at trot, with a cavalry detachment close behind; all day in the sun and then all night on the great mountain as black as a stranded whale that huge man, that hero lying down on the mountaintop, would keep watch and contemplate the stars. Where are you, children? Hebdomeros is in love with Louise, the maid from the house opposite; he has put on his new suit; the bells are ringing in the parish church towers and spring smiles on the vegetable gardens. Spring, spring! Funeral procession, gruesome spectacle. Corpses in tuxedos, lying in their open coffins, are lined up on the beaches in the south; the air is filled with the obsessive smell of lemon, which, like garlic and onions, makes food indigestible; and here are oranges with their obscene flowers, unmentionably symbolic. Where are you bound for, you with the coat trimmed with an astrakhan collar? You who are the prototype of the eternal traveler, always ready to protect the sick child from the grasping hands of bandits on this train that stinks of cattle soaked by an August downpour. Where are you going, helmeted warrior with the sinister face? Heart of steel with windows opening onto villages clinging to the mountainsides like vultures' nests, where the avaricious innkeeper indicates with his red hand the whole sweep of the valley and the river running through it, now opaque, now crystal-clear, like the life of man. Is it then necessary to renounce one's place, and when one has paid for a first-class ticket to insist on traveling second class despite the mild protests of the conductor? But it's a lake as vast as the sea and which, like the sea, has dangerous fits of temper; beware then of drowning, and if the motorboats rush to your rescue, then you will know what it means to be reborn on this summer afternoon when the sidewalks, washed by the shower, reflect the lights from the shopwindows so well you'd think you were in Venice; and that charming city built like an amphitheater around the lake? Oh, but a different lake this time, a peaceful unruffled lake, a consoling lake. And when the weather is sultry, and the first heavy drops of rain fall on the water as the storm begins, then the big fish bite by the dozen and you haul them in two at a time, big and black, on the end of your Florentine line! You call that the *slaughter of the innocents*? But at this point Hebdomeros protested; paying no attention to the passengers who made fun of him as they crossed the gangway, nudging their wives and roaring with laughter, he confessed his dislike of biblical scenes, which he described as immoral and lewd; he maintained that behind the idea of depicting Christ as a lamb lurked a sensual urge of a particular kind, and he concluded with a declamation in praise of cafés with red plush divans and ceiling decorations in the style of the 1880s.

"There," Hebdomeros would say, in a voice strained a little by emotion, "you feel protected from the dangers of the outside world; no matter though the ruthless enemy sends his elite regiments right up to the gates of the city, or comets with deleterious tails appear on the horizon, or couples of lions spitting flames walk through the middle of the town, or iron-beaked birds infest the trees in the city squares, or buzzing insects swarm down on the steaming feces of cholera victims, once you are in that café it's all the same to you. Once there, you are safe and if you stand on tiptoe and look over the transom you can see the enemy ships dropping anchor off the deserted shore and launches crammed with warriors being rowed swiftly toward the bank. And then a kind of solidarity springs up among these refugees; each has his own task and his appointed place; the women and children are placed in safety in the back of the shop behind the large boxes and the crates of canned food. It is there that all those unfitted for dangerous and tiring work spend their time preparing food, which consists of preserved horse meat, biscuits, honey, and coffee which is always drunk very hot and spiced; they also see that the weapons are carefully cleaned and that shoes and clothes are mended; the youngest go off in search of game, as provisions have to be laid in for the winter; the rainy season has already begun; the continual rains have soaked the ground and the paths are slippery; puddles are forming in the rather tall grass, where, in places, daisies and cornflowers make a timid appearance, just enough to brighten this bit of path and throw a poetic note in the way of the zealous students who work with joy and perseverance in austere classrooms where everything is only promise; the polar bear splashing about among the ice blocks or fighting with a walrus for a mangled fish, and the ostrich fleeing desperately from the Arab horseman; and then the bridges and castles with their numberless turrets, and the ruins where thousands of crows have made their nests." Hebdomeros thought that he was safe in this cabin, as he had noticed no trace of human life in the vicinity, but despite the reassuring appearances he was still wary, he was not a man to trust appearances; he remembered how many times in early childhood he had been deceived by appearances, so he remained on his guard, and when night fell he slept with one eye open, keeping his leaded cane and automatic pistol within reach; often he did not even take off his shoes and slept half clothed, ready if necessary to face any unpleasant surprise. But winter passed without any unusual occurrences. Already the air grew warmer and the plants turned green on the plain; the goatherds had come down from the surrounding mountains and played cheerful tunes on their long copper flutes; spring was in the air; in this Nordic country it arrived suddenly, with the striking effect of a stage decor appearing behind a rising curtain; an air of symbolism floated over nature; hundreds of tiny waterfalls, fed by the melting snows, tumbled down the mountainsides; angels with enormous wings, like those of eagles but interwoven with feathers as white and soft as goose feathers, sat by the wayside, one hand on the huge milestones that bore the sculptured likeness of two-headed Janus surmounted by a male sex organ;

the angels were watching with a melancholy air the couples who moved off arm in arm beneath the almond trees in blossom. Everywhere banners with flamboyant lettering; toward the east, groups of huntsmen with their hounds were crossing the mountainous volcanic region in fierce pursuit of the few survivors of that almost extinct race of pachyderms. High in the sky the vultures wheeled around, and now and again they would drop or rise in the air, fearing some ill-fated shot from the earth, but they never lost sight of the huntsmen. Their aim was clear: to wait until a mammoth had been killed and cut up and then to gorge themselves on the remains when the last huntsman and hound had disappeared behind the rocks. In spite of the presence of the vultures and animal bones which lay whitening here and there in the grayness of the rocks, the landscape was not particularly wild or desolate; large mining facilities were dotted all over it; chimneys smoked and wagons ran along tiny rails; bearded engineers, their faces red from the heat, hurried here and there and took advantage of their rare moments of leisure to go fishing or practice shooting at empty bottles. Their only entertainment was an evening at the puppet show. This idea had come to a sculptor with a head like an Assyrian king who boasted of having been the pupil of a fashionable master and who enjoyed quite a reputation in his own social circle for playing the flute, which he did, by the way, rather badly. These puppet shows were not as quiet and naive as might be thought; at times the puppet master, a hysterical man subject to epileptic fits, began, even as he manipulated his little cardboard men with their Cretan eyes, to let out such howls that the foremen, waking with a start, jumped out of bed and ran for the sirens. The hyenas then abandoned the half-unearthed cadavers and fled toward the nearby mountains. The drivers, who dozed on their wagons and only half opened an eye at each bump, jumped to their feet, seized by a wild panic, made their whips whistle, and set their beasts off at full tilt; seen thus at night these wagons rushing off at top speed looked almost apocalyptic. Leaving the monstrous station of this metropolis where close to eight million men bustled about from morning to night without rhyme or reason, Hebdomeros set off toward that region of nocturnal celebrations which, at the very heart of the city, constituted a world apart. Indeed, it had its boundaries and frontiers, its laws and statutes, and it would hardly have been surprising if zealous customs officers stood guard at its gates to ask if you had anything to declare. At the edge of this ineffable district the traffic of the great city came to a halt; it was here that the convulsive movement of the vehicles and the coming and going of the busy pedestrians came at last to die, as a wave dies on the beach. *Happiness Has Its Rights*: these words would be seen in lights on the main gateway which formed the central part of a gigantic triumphal arch upon which the figures of women, carved in wood and painted in bright pastel shades, were blowing, like obstinate tritons, into the long trumpets of fame. The fortresses which rose beside it, the refuge of those whom fortune neglects but whom the gratitude and kindness of men does not forget, kept vigil alone in the darkness; their solemn arches were silent in the profound peace which sleep demands; the hour was well advanced into the dark night; the world slept buried in an immense tranquility, and even so the storm which agitated the troubled heart of Hebdomeros seemed calmed at last. The glory of the past, the vanity of human heroism, and those pyramids that the fear of oblivion compelled the directors of public affairs to have built by indifferent employees who while constructing them had other things on their minds, of the fiancée or wife who awaited them down there, far from the noise and the smoke, in their peaceful homes near a window open on the coolness of the garden where thousands of fireflies striped the darkness with phosphorescent streaks. Thus it is in vain that processions of kings advance along the main country roads; seen from afar their solemn aspect seems much diminished, alas! Were it not for the glint of the weapons brandished by the cavalry escort, one would have thought them a troop of tattered gypsies going to beg bread under the implacable sun and the constant menace of Molossians with mud-caked fur that the cruel peasants set at their heels. If one believes that from pity can love be born, then there exists a whole promising array of inexpressible feelings which appears on the vast horizon of Hebdomeros's life. Infinite nostalgias and sudden bursts of emotion which, in his imagination heightened by the sleepless nights in the trains of the state railways, took on the hieroglyphic form of a giant greyhound with a body of an inexpressible length, bounding in a rigid leap across the world, passing like a missile over the motley pattern of towns, over the tamed forests where each tree has its name and its history, over the fields whose vast hollow is made fertile by more than one seed which the provident farmer sows at the opportune moment; and Hebdomeros's compassion turned toward all humanity; toward the loquacious man and the taciturn, toward the rich who suffer and toward the poor, but the deepest compassion he felt for those men who eat alone in restaurants, especially when they are seated near a window so that the passersby, cruel and disrespectful, true phantoms living in another atmosphere, can defile with their brazen look the virginal purity, the tender chastity, the infinite tenderness, the ineffable melancholy of this moment they are living, a moment above all solitary, covering them with a shame so gentle and so poignant that one doesn't understand why all the personnel of the premises, with the manager and the cashier, with the furniture, the tablecloths, the wine jugs, and all the dishes down to the saltcellars and the smallest objects, do not dissolve in an endless flood of tears.

The great hypostases which accompanied these telluric upheavals were followed by unforgettable spectacles, at which Hebdomeros never failed to be present. Millions and millions of warriors invaded the country, passing through the vineyards; one might have said that they oozed from the cracks in the rocks, through these mountains modeled in relief, a hypothetical ordnance survey map, riddled with caves and which the uniform light coming from the ceiling made appear still more unreal. *Myrmidons! Myrmidons!* ... repeated from echo to echo, this cry reverberated along the deserted beaches, as in the Tertiary epoch. Above the peristyle the sky was clear and of a deep blue; barometers in offices were fair and steady, despair to the navigator on the motionless caravel in the middle of the ocean. At other points of the globe, where those sinister lakes, with water still and black whose depths had never been sounded, opened their disquieting eye turned toward the sky like the eye of the *Uranoscopus*, which the simple fisherman charmingly calls the parson-fish, clouds heavy as rocks and black as night were torn apart by the sporadic flight of jagged lightning; then the rain fell and fell without end, in long packed strands, in perpendicular sheaves, on the surface of the lake which began to seethe; water into water; hydropic philosophers, demigods become poseurs through wishing to appear simple and unaffected, tried to be clever and, after having hung their clothes on the quicklime-spattered branches of a barren fig tree on the bank, they went into the water *so they wouldn't get wet*, they said, and sometimes they waited whole days for these strange storms to break in order to have the chance to make this subtle joke. Hebdomeros was revolted, for at the same time he was thinking of something else. "Eloquence of the past," he said, addressing his friends, "before these indiscreet displays, before these sumptuous still lifes where bananas and pineapples fall in an avalanche to the flanks of disemboweled deer and polychrome pheasants, before that provocative presumptuousness of well-being, before that gigantic insult, that fantastic slap in the face at poverty and sobriety, I have seen vengeance grinning in the shadow. Then among the overturned stools and the fragments of bottles the tablecloths strewing the floor wrap themselves like elephant traps around the feet of the hurrying waiters loaded with dishes, thus causing real disasters; the busy servants topple over, leading to terrible wreckage accompanied by a flood of sauces of all colors on which float, like abandoned ships, the roasted and shriveled bodies of chickens." Hebdomeros could go no further; he rose like those shadows which rise on the damp walls of cells when a lantern is placed on the ground; he rose and spoke in a voice grave but strange, as if he did not see the two thousand six hundred and seventy-five faces of those men who came there to hear him and who kept their eyes fixed on him. But at length he returned to reality and talked of September mornings on the sacred hill which overlooked the city; at once voices arose:—The acropolis, the acropolis!—"No," he replied with a sly smile, "there is no question, this time, of *a crow*, or of *Paulus*; though there is indeed a Pericles, it is not the one of whom you instinctively think, he who was felled by the implacable plague at the end of a hot summer day, and who was the affectionate friend of painters, sculptors, architects, and poets; the Pericles I present to you is one-eyed, and to hide that infirmity he wears his helmet pulled down on his head as far as the middle of his nose; but even so he has style and a certain elegance, especially when he throws his chlamys over his left shoulder with a careless gesture; his legs, long and knock-kneed, far from making him ridiculous, recall, apart from the anachronism, the old picadors whom age has sent from the arena but for which they retain a nostalgia; he holds a coin in his left hand and contemplates for a long time, in silence, his head tilted slightly backward, with a compassionate eye (in this case it can be said since he was one-eyed) the profile of a woman engraved on one side of it." Among the drumlike shapes of the fallen columns where, at evening when the square is deserted, huge dysenteric mares come to graze eagerly on the tender chamomile blossoms which flower in the shadow of the glorious ruins, the faithful, those whom fright, selfishness, and shameful cowardice have not conquered, those who have preferred to brave fear and to look death in the face, firmly planted on their armor-clad legs, rather than submit to the shame of disguising themselves as women, as pregnant peasants, and as wet nurses and mingling with that crowd of two-legged ewes to escape in crammed and overladen boats which threaten to sink with each stroke of the oar, were all in their places. At the moment they remained lying on the ground around Hebdomeros in idle, magnificent attitudes and listened to him speak, like pirates listening to their chief recounting the appalling stories of boardings and combat at night. When evening came the long shafts of light, which the searchlights installed by the rebels on the surrounding heights beamed in all directions, greatly disturbed this noble society of ascetic warriors and disabused gentlemen; those who had the luck to find themselves in proximity to a pile of ruins which in falling had happened to form a kind of grotto were less disturbed by the play of the reflectors; but the others, whose only resource was to lean their aching backs against the hard, cold drum of a column, were more than likely to spend a sleepless night. It sometimes happened that certain among them turned their backs to the sea, for the sight of the shore did not interest them at all. This was, after all, their milieu, their world, and these fishermen accustomed to nautical mythology were not at all impressed by what was going on around them, rather were they intrigued by the presence of the luxury hotels lighted on every floor and shining like beacons on the high, sheer cliffs at the foot of which long waves died away silently. The windows were open; on the balconies, on the terraces, the rich guests in evening clothes had come out, drawn by the whispering of all those sea-gods stranded below on the dark beach.

Hebdomeros and his companions, leaving this place where there was nothing more for them to do, entered the suburbs that were like the backstage of the city. In fact, it was there that each of these personages, whose activity so strongly attracted the attention of everyone, went to apply makeup, to prepare himself, to rehearse his role, like actors who await the cue to go onstage to recite with all the skill their masters have taught them that which they know by heart or almost, in order to play this role on the dusty boards, on those boards which, in spite of new ideas and the evolution of tastes and customs, are always somehow dirty and shameful. More than once Hebdomeros, when he meditated on so many unsolved enigmas, asked himself this question: Why is there always something shameful about the theater?— He never succeeded in giving himself a satisfactory answer. Now it sometimes happened that finding himself alone in his room, plunged in his meditations, the twilight descended gently; his three friends always left him toward six in the evening; they went off cheerfully, singing, their gait accelerated by the steep slope which went down toward the marketplace. Hebdomeros remained alone up there in that house where, ten years before, he had rented a small room shabbily furnished. Later, by dint of economy, saving on all sides, sustained by that will which, under an aspect of weariness and weakness, had always dominated his life, he had succeeded in renting the whole house and in dispossessing the original tenants, not to avenge himself for the bad treatment to which they had subjected him on many occasions, but to punish them for their meanness; he considered this a just act. "Justice above all," he said, seating himself at the table to consume a modest meal which he prepared himself; this meal consisted, most often, of a scrawny bird (a kind of undernourished lark) which an octogenarian hunter who was at the same time his next-door neighbor brought to him each day. This old man had a worship for hunting which came close to mysticism and obsession. Up at dawn, he whistled for his old dog, who followed him, yawning, after stretching hard enough to dislocate his bones. Thus every evening Hebdomeros bought a bird from him which he did not eat until the following evening, for he liked, in his moments of leisure, to paint still lifes of game. So he placed the dead bird on a table with a napkin; sometimes he also placed cotton batting around it, as if it were snow, which made him think of hunting in winter and the happy gatherings of hunters in inns, seated near the fireplaces where logs blazed, drinking cheerfully and smoking long pipes. At the dinner hour he plucked the bird and put it in a small pot with some goat's butter and a little salt; while it cooked he turned it around, sticking it with a fork and always repeating out loud the same sentence: "It must feel the heat. It must feel the heat." If someone knocked at the door just as he was about to sit down to eat, he would still have enough courage to invite them to share his meal, which, apart from the tiny roast bird, consisted of an end of rye bread and a spoonful of blueberry jam; with it he drank fresh beer yeast dissolved in filtered water with a little sugar. He had a moral theory about different dishes, in fact about food in general, which earned him the antipathy and exasperated sarcasm of many of his contemporaries. He divided dishes into two categories: moral and immoral. He was utterly disgusted by the sight of certain restaurants where gourmets go to satisfy the obscene desires of their gastrointestinal apparatus, and his soul was filled with a righteous and holy indignation. Like Orestes pursued by the Furies he fled from those who ate lobsters, first taking a nutcracker to break the paws and pincers of these hideous, armored monsters, and then sucking at them with bestial delight. But what upset him most was to see, at the beginning of a meal, the oyster addicts swallowing this disgusting mollusk with all the accompanying paraphernalia of carefully buttered slices of black bread, small glasses of special white wine, thin slivers of lemon, etc....; and the whole ritual seasoned with revolting theories and obscene explanations of the effect lemon has on the mollusk, which, when it is still alive, contracts, or long, ridiculous harangues about the aroma of oysters, which makes you think of the sea and waves bashing against the cliffs and similar nonsense that only someone totally devoid of all sense of decency and self-control would find amusing. He also found very immoral the habit of eating ice cream in cafés, and the whole idea of putting cubes of ice in drinks. Beaten egg whites and whipped cream were also, in his view, harmful, impure substances. Another thing that he thought was extremely immoral and ought to be stamped out vigorously was the exaggerated and instinctive partiality, often verging on voracity, that women, especially, have for raw vegetables: pickles, cucumbers, artichokes preserved in vinegar, etc.... He considered strawberries and figs the most immoral of fruits.

Being served in the morning for breakfast with fresh figs covered with crushed ice was, for Hebdomeros, an offense so serious as to deserve, according to his code, a sentence varying from ten to fifteen years of detention. Most punishable, also, in his eyes, was the act of eating strawberries and cream; he could not understand how sensible people could commit such obscene acts and how they had the courage to do so in public, in front of other people, instead of hiding the shame of their unspeakable actions in the depths of the darkest rooms and double-locking the doors as if about to commit rape or incest. He put it all down to human stupidity, which he considered as immense and eternal as the universe and in which he had unshakable faith. Unshakable faith! He should have liked to nurse it, this faith, swollen every day by fresh examples; he should have liked to nurse it as a hepatic patient nurses his liver at the hot cholagogic springs; *acquae calidae*; Caesar, dyspeptic and in love, surrounded by his legions in the conquered valley. No one read the hymn he composed that evening, neither his most faithful friends nor even that virgin with the ardent glance and the royal walk to whom the hymn was dedicated; he feared *what-will-people-say*, he hated these social circles that were as indiscreet as they were obtuse. Now the trees which had invaded the rooms and corridors of his house moved off slowly toward the south; they emigrated in groups, in families and tribes; they were already far off, and with them died away the thousand voices of the mysterious forest and its disturbing odor. An aged, taciturn servant whom Hebdomeros called Eumenides was sweeping out the ruins that were still strewn about the floor, and before this new life, before the magnificent panorama spread out like a map of the world, he suddenly *saw* the Oceans. Like the Colossus of Rhodes, but a Colossus of Rhodes infinitely enlarged in a dream, his feet at the end of his outspread legs touched different lands; between his left toes Mexican bandits were pursuing each other like half-starved wild animals around overheated rocks during the dog days, while the right foot was treading upon the pure, white regions up there among the polar bears, fat weasel-faced old men nodding their heads in front of the notched, jagged crenellations of the glaciers that rose up like the ruins of famous cathedrals destroyed by cannon; while on the threshold of their stinking huts lined with sealskins, Eskimos all wrapped up in furs politely offered their wives to excited explorers. Once again the flares rose silently in the distance into the great, dark night; compact groups of philosophers and warriors, like polycephalic blocks in soft, luminous colors, held mysterious secret meetings in corners of the low-ceilinged rooms, just where the ornamental moldings joining the walls to the ceiling formed a right angle. "I don't like the look of those faces," burst out one of Hebdomeros's youngest disciples, to whom he replied: "All right, I understand, or at least I can guess what you are thinking; you would have preferred the well-behaved phantoms of a puritanical society restricted by its laws, that avoids speeches referring to microbes and surgical instruments and turns pale with fright when tactless people use expressions like *the firstborn son of a previous marriage*, or discuss midwives and methods of childbirth, you would have preferred the company of these phantoms on an enclosed veranda when the long, silent lightning streaks flash, quick and regular like the batting of eyelids, and herald the storm approaching in the distance. Indeed, soon the rumbling of thunder, muffled at first and barely perceptible, is growing louder; gusts of wind sweep through the garden, whirling up the dead leaves and the magazines left on the cane chairs, and then heavy, warm drops of rain begin to fall on the dusty paths with the noise of a finger tapping against thick, taut material. 'Shut the windows! Shut the windows!' cries the lady of the house, rushing madly through the rooms like Niobe obsessed by the sight of her children bristling with darts; then, young man, one sees this inexplicable sight: strange hens, completely plucked bare, run around the dining table on their long legs, panic-stricken, like miniature ostriches; funeral violinists put away their instruments hurriedly in cases that look like babies' coffins; portraits move in their frames and pictures on the wall drop to the ground; ghostly cooks, prototypes of assassins, climb stealthily up to the second floor to the bedrooms of those distinguished-looking and bald old men who, armed with their ivory-headed canes, prepare to die with dignity, so that their nephews will not have to blush when referring to them. You would have preferred that, rash young man," added Hebdomeros, still addressing his young disciple with a meaningful smile. "But think, rather, of the fine clear days by the seashore, think of the Immortals blessing those who love them and who, wearing golden helmets and silver breastplates, set off in ships to die over there on the other bank; for they know that this is the best way to return later to their loved ones and live there without malice and without remorse; it is true that they return only as ghosts; but, as the proverb says, better to return as a ghost than never at all; think over all that and don't trust appearances, then you'll no longer have the unfortunate inspiration to make observations like the one I have just heard." Hebdomeros turned his steps again toward the rivers with the concrete banks, toward the decaying palaces whose domes and weather vanes rose up under the ever-fleeing clouds. This forbidding place whose solemn door was closed at the moment ought to have saddened him, but the recollection of what he had seen there during moments spent in the midst of a scattered and indifferent public was quite enough to console him. He saw, arising slowly out of the chiaroscuro of his memory and little by little defining themselves in his mind, the shapes of those temples and sanctuaries built in plaster that stand at the foot of sheltering mountains and rocks through which ran narrow passes that made one strangely aware not only of the unknown worlds nearby but also of those distant horizons heavy with adventure that ever since his unhappy childhood Hebdomeros had always loved. A magic word shone in the air like the cross of Constantine and multiplied itself in space to the edge of the horizon like the ads for a toothpaste: *Delphoï! Delphoï!* A soft sighing noise like laurel bushes bent over by the autumn winds passed through the warm air and, on the other bank, just opposite the sacred place where the golden columns of the Temple of Immorality gleamed in the rays of a sun nailed to the center of the ceiling so that it could not sink down, appeared, hanging on the wall, the very sad paintings of epochs long past. "It's to maintain the balance," the guide was saying, "for too much happiness is harmful." And so Hebdomeros saw Christ insulted by the crowd and then dragged by the legionaries before Pilate; and he also saw the Flood: masses of water swirling over the plains, and women, with muscles like Titans, clinging to the last remaining rocks while elephants stood out, silhouetted black against the livid flashes of lightning, waving their terrified trunks in the face of the tempest. But was it really worthwhile evoking all that? Insomnia in the suffocating night and the tiger's eyes shining in the bedroom near the closed mosquito net. The moonlight was so soft that the mountains seemed very near; the night gods were whispering at the frontiers of the town, there where the last pavements are like harbor quays before the sea of fields and meadows; you could go on board, set off, and sail at leisure on the yellow waves of ripe wheat or on the green ripples of fresh grass; those who remain behind in the last café, over there at the end of this part of the town that juts out like a promontory into the sea of fields, those who remain wave their handkerchiefs and raise their hands in salute: Be happy! *Lebe wohl!* May fortune smile on you! Good luck! But behind the polychrome waves of this sea decked out with red poppies and timid cornflowers the boat disappears slowly as if it were being swallowed up in a very calm sea; the sails, bellying out in the spring wind, are still visible, then they too disappear and peace descends once more over the countryside and birds that had stopped singing for a moment, before this unexpected sight, burst out again into joyful warbling. Now the thousand noises of nature spring up again like the bustle of street life momentarily halted by a passing funeral procession; the country is again full of life and gaiety and shows all this off without embarrassment or remorse; in front of the farms whose doors are wreathed with flowers the peasants and peasant women, heated by the consumption of fermented drinks, dance in a circle around slippery poles and with sharp cries throw into the air their beribboned hats. With his arms crossed like a stern tribune watching an orgy, Hebdomeros stared thoughtfully at these noisy manifestations of innocent joy; he was thinking: "These men are happy, or at least they seem to be, for on that subject there would be much to say as well; but happy or unhappy, or simply undisturbed, one thing is certain, that is that the famous *tempting demon* who haunts us others, men of sensibility and intellect, has never come to sit at their table or their bedside; he has never followed them as they go off to work at sunrise, sickle on shoulder, watching the flight of the lark that rises in the sky like the white ping-pong ball on a jet of water in a shooting booth; still less does he follow them in the evening when they return tired to their cottages, while the crows, after gorging themselves on rotting carcasses lying at the bottom of dried-up riverbeds, in regular couples regain the neighboring mountains with a slow rhythmic flight, calling now and again in the low croak that I have always liked. And we know what it means, that demon who snickers constantly at your side; you are far from town, you think yourself as free and easy as a schoolboy who has played hooky; you are sitting on a bench near a deserted path shaded by trees whose thick foliage checks the burning rays of the sun and forces them to filter harmlessly through and pick out on the road the perforated notes of an aerophone disk; you think yourself easy and free and indulge in dreams and memories of the past, recollecting the faces of women you have loved and the most important events, sad or happy, in your life; you think yourself easy and free when all of a sudden you realize that you are not alone; *someone* is still sitting on your bench; yes, this gentleman dressed with an outmoded elegance whose face reminds you vaguely of certain photographs of Napoleon III and also of Anatole France at the time of *The Red Lily*, this gentleman who is looking at you with a sly laugh, it's always he, the *tempting demon*. In a while, when you get up, long after he has disappeared, and you set off along the dusty path, he will leap out from behind a tree, uncannily imitating the barking of a dog, and if you lose your patience and begin to hurl stones at him with all your strength, he will rush off across the fields like a madman, shouting insults and accusing you in front of the villagers of the worst misdemeanors, even of raping little girls and setting fire to farms." This long soliloquy had made Hebdomeros rather tired and sad; the weather was still very fine; on the sunny heights green trees were spaced out at intervals, mingling the various shades of their foliage; the clearings were carpeted with very green young grass where children played and shouted happily; houses that were modest but which looked clean, cheerful, and inviting poked their pointed roofs up between the trees; everything was at rest in the light. Yet, nearby, events of an unheard-of solemnity followed one another with the fatality dictated by the goddess History as she sat on a cloud with a book lying open on her knee; portly Cabinet Ministers were shaking hands with and looking into the eyes of monarchs whose torsos were mosaicked with medals and ribbons, while below in the harbor iron-plated vessels made their weapons thunder and hoisted up the poles and masts their flags and pennants; at that moment Mercury, who was flying over the spot, looked down, and when the burst of cannon fire echoed through the valley he raised his staff in one hand and waved it with joy.

Where to return? To the mines? Hebdomeros instinctively avoided these unhealthy areas where fever reigned unchecked all the year round and innkeepers place sulphate of quinine on the tables as elsewhere one places pepper and salt. Rather the boredom of a life adjusted to the hands of a watch but essentially logical and not lacking in poetry, full of unshed tears; the life on this road lined with houses from each of which rose the lament of pianos tormented by adolescents practicing their morning scales. All that would have been quite normal, after all, and Hebdomeros, not to mention his friends and disciples, would hardly have been averse to taking a few days' rest in these monotonous, reposing surroundings, but something unusual drew their attention and made them realize that things were not as normal as they had at first thought. In front of each house was a small garden with cane benches and chaise longues; in each garden an enormous old man, made entirely of stone, was stretched out on one of the chaise longues; Hebdomeros was astonished that the chairs were able to support such a weight, and said as much to his companions, but when they drew nearer they saw that the armchairs which they had taken to be made of cane were in fact all metal, and the interweaving of the steel rods, painted a straw color, had been so well conceived that they could have withstood far greater pressures. These old men *were alive*, yes, alive, but only just; there was a very faint glow of life in their faces and the upper part of their bodies; at times their eyes would move, but their heads remained motionless; it was as if they were suffering from an eternal stiff neck and wished to avoid the slightest movement from fear of reawakening the pain. Sometimes a light flush spread over their cheeks and in the evening when the sun had disappeared behind the nearby wooded mountains they talked from one garden to the next, telling stories of long ago. They spoke of the days of hunts for roe deer and grouse in the forests that were damp and dark even at noon; they recalled how many times they had rushed upon one another, holding their rifles by the end of the barrel and brandishing them like clubs or grasping their hunting knives in their fists. The eternal cause of these brawls was a dead animal that two hunters had both claimed to have killed. But one evening the big stone men no longer spoke; specialists who were hastily called to examine them found that the tiny glimmer of life that had kept them alive until then had disappeared; even the top of the cranium was cold and their eyes had closed; then it was decided to have them taken away so that they shouldn't uselessly encumber the little gardens of the villas; a man who called himself a sculptor was summoned; it was a man with a disquieting manner and a horrible squint; he mingled in his conversation stupid puns and coarse jokes and his breath stank of brandy from yards away. He arrived with a case full of mallets of various sizes and set to work right away; one after the other the old stone men were broken up and thrown into the valley, which soon began to look like a battlefield after the battle. The tide broke upon these pitiful fragments; down there behind the black cliffs whose silhouette looked like the figures of gothic apostles the moon rose; a pale, northern moon; it was fleeing on the clouds across the sky; Hebdomeros and his friends stood like shipwrecked men on a raft, looking toward the south; they knew that over there whence came the gale, beyond the stormy sea that threw up great mountains of foam onto the shore, lay Africa; yes, towns whitened by the intense heat of the sun, thirst, and dysentery, but also cool oases where you wish for nothing more, and a kind of strange, gentle wisdom that falls from the top of palm trees along with the ripe dates, in the chaste hours of early morning; but they must not think of it; Hebdomeros watched the clouds coming from the south and scudding away toward the north where the sky was still bright; soon this part of the heavens too was covered in clouds, thin ones at first that came at intervals like great black veils trailing from some invisible hand up there and then denser ones that came closer together; in no time at all the whole sky was black. "Even so, we should go north," said Hebdomeros to his companions, who approved the idea. "It is true, friends," he went on, "that the North is a little like the West, whereas the South is a little like the East; I would advise you to beware of the South and the East, for they are deleterious and corrosive lands. To the North lie life and happiness, beauty and light; there is joy in work and sleep without remorse; if you have something to say or something to show, say it and show it in the North and the West, you will have more chance there than anywhere else of being understood and rewarded for your pains. But that does not mean, friends, that you ought never to visit the South and the East; the day will come when not only will you go there but also will stay there; however it is by way of the North that one must go; these are strongholds to be taken through a ruse, not by frontal attacks, which result only in failure and loss of men and equipment; in the wide world the inimical things far outnumber the favorable ones so you must have sound tactics and good strategy and know how to combat them using not only your courage but also your knowledge and your wits; courage is not sufficient. That your friends and relations, or even people whom you have never heard of but who know you and follow your activities with attention and sympathy may one day say: 'He went down fighting,' is not sufficient; all that you will see in these words is regret for your wild youth wasted away in the pursuit of easy pleasures until the moment you reached maturity, when deeper layers of reason force you to accept discipline and work, and drive you toward ever finer and greater achievements which henceforth bathe your life in the eternal light of fame. That the civil engineers sweat in shirt-sleeves among drains and pipelines in the heat of the dog days shouldn't be for you a cause of remorse and a desire to follow in their footsteps; if suspiciously tepid water flows from the faucets in your house, if the flies set upon your food and if the whey and sauces turn bad in the cupboards, think of hunting in the polar regions, think of the sea lions biting fiercely into the wooden crafts that pitch alarmingly; and think also of the great pine forests on the high mountainsides at the hour the sun disappears slowly in the clear air behind the rocky summits, opening, as it sinks, the doors to the fresh winds that give new life to the plants and flowers and bring the animals out from the lairs and dens they had fled to from the heat of the midday sun. Think also of those blessed towns over which eternal fog and mist spread a kindly veil, where in full daylight albino children can look straight at the orb of the sun, where men have fair skin and blue eyes and where artists work long hours on portraits and seascapes which can be examined, once finished, with a magnifying glass." Hebdomeros's friends and disciples leaned against balustrades or lay on the ground as they listened; following the period at the fireside they now found themselves on the interior patrol paths of the battlements, protected by thick walls; around about them the pillars alternated sometimes in style and the lancet arches rose on all sides in harmonious curves. When he had finished his long speech, they applauded and then got to their feet to look down at the little harbor where two frigates flying unfamiliar colors had anchored that day at dawn. At present the sailors were repairing the sails, making lifeboats to replace those damaged by the storm and preparing salt provisions, while talkative and long-haired specialists quarreled loudly among themselves as they installed scientific equipment on the blocks of the breakwater under construction. The position of this town, which Hebdomeros called the most happily situated in the universe, at the mouth of a river which ran through it and fertilized its countryside and which was easily navigable right up to the fish-filled lake where it originated, delighted these perspicacious young men who were given to lyrical flights of the imagination. Meanwhile, night had fallen and the scene changed. As sometimes happens in dreams the gentle charm of this landscape faded gradually away to give place to the unsightly outline of unfriendly rocks which fog and factory smoke had masked during the day but which now loomed up suddenly in the shadows. The crater of a volcano began to spew out whirlwinds of smoke and small yellow and bluish flames; the valley's luxuriant vegetation disappeared into darkness. The lake lay in a hollow surrounded by steep walls; the natives declared that at the middle of the lake they had tried in vain to sound its depths, which probably disappeared in the bowels of the earth; strange tales were told, otherwise serious-minded men claimed to have seen in the dead of night monsters from the Tertiary period roaming on the surface. The fact is that no one dared to venture forth into the middle of the lake; moreover, a line of small vermilion red buoys marked the beginning of the area where the depth probe no longer touched bottom. Hebdomeros was more decided than ever to leave this land which hid behind a deceptive facade of peacefulness and fertility strange snares and terrors. As long as the sun was shining all went well, but once night fell you saw the other side of the coin; yet the inhabitants were by no means uncivilized and their tastes were quite refined, as can be seen from the following menu served to Hebdomeros and his friends in a restaurant where they went for dinner:

CARROT SOUP

ARTICHOKES

GIGOT OF MUTTON

MASHED POTATOES

SEMOLINA PUDDING

STEWED PRUNES

Still, one couldn't pass one's nights in the fear of meeting an ichthyosaur or of being awakened from a deep sleep by the roar of a volcano. Hebdomeros would rather have put up with the opposite: living in anguish during the day, but once night fell, once the bolts were drawn, the blinds lowered, and the doors shut, to be able to retire in perfect safety and peace of mind. He looked upon sleep as something sacred and very gentle and he did not allow his peace to be disturbed by anyone or anything. He expressed a similar respect for the children of sleep, namely dreams; that was why he had engraved at the foot of his bed an image of Mercury *oneiropomp*, that is, the bringer of dreams, for, as everyone knows, Mercury was engaged by Jupiter not only with exercising the profession of *psychopomp*, he who guides the souls of the dead to the world beyond, but also of bringing dreams to the sleep of the living. On the wall Hebdomeros had hung a most curious picture painted by

one of his friends, an artist of great talent who unfortunately had died very young. He was an intrepid swimmer
and once, having wished to attempt crossing a river in
flood, he was swept by the current and, despite his own
efforts and the efforts of those who tried to save him, he
disappeared in the eddies. The picture he had painted
depicted Mercury as a shepherd, holding a crook in place
of his staff; he was driving before him toward the darkness of sleep his flock of dreams. The picture was very
well composed, for in the background in the distance,
behind Mercury and his flock, one saw a sunny countryside, towns, harbors, men going about their business,
peasants working in the fields, in short, life; while surrounding Mercury and his strange flock all was dark and
desolate as though they had entered a vast tunnel. And
also because of dreams, Hebdomeros refrained from
eating fava beans at dinner; in this he agreed with Py-
thagoras, who maintains that fava beans cause dreams
to be dark and confused. Hebdomeros sincerely regret-
ted the death of the young artist; he kept a photograph
taken a few days before the reckless attempt that was to
cost him his life; this photograph shows the artist from
in front, his face adorned with a black beard that contrasted with the almost infantile expression of his features. "He had a passion for beards," said Hebdomeros
whenever his friends asked him for details about the
young artist's life; "he loved certain aspects of the past,
of the relatively recent past that we find in the portraits
of our parents in their youth. All the same, he used to

shave, though for the photograph he had let his beard grow, as film actors sometimes do to look more convincing in roles where this ornament to the male features is indispensable; but they are wrong, quite wrong, for a false beard always looks more real on the screen than a true one, just as a film set made of wood and cardboard is always more 'authentic' than a natural one. But try telling that to the film directors who spend their time looking for fine sites and picturesque vistas; alas, they understand nothing!" Hebdomeros fell silent and stared thoughtfully at the gentle arabesques of an oriental carpet he had just bought. Now and then during his reveries he passed his hand over his forehead as if to push sad thoughts and unwelcome images from his mind and raising his head he said: "Let us talk further about him, this young artist who fell victim to his own daring. Surely if he had had full awareness of his own worth, he would not have risked his life in that way, out of bravado, to achieve an athletic feat that others with better training and greater resistance would certainly have brought off successfully; he would have worked away quietly, carefully avoiding dangers and risks. With regard to perfumes, he only liked Eau de Lubin, and occasionally Eau de Cologne; but he used to say that, from a certain point of view, Eau de Lubin had a more evocative scent." Just as Hebdomeros said these last words a burst of cannon fire echoed throughout the harbor; at once numerous pigeons, frightened by the explosion, whirled past the balcony; instinctively everyone pulled out their watch, thinking it was noon, but Hebdomeros put out a restraining hand; "No, my friends, we have not yet reached the middle of the day; the cannon shot you have just heard does not mean that the sun in space, the hands on the clock, and the shadows on the sundials have reached that fateful point which some say indicates the hour of ghosts far more interesting and complicated than those which ordinarily appear before us at the stroke of midnight in deserted graveyards or in the lonely ruins of a haunted castle under the pallid light of the moon as it bursts through the storm clouds, ghosts that you and I know well, having seen them often since our earliest childhood. The cannon shot you have just heard, my friends, is simply announcing the arrival in our port of the steamer *Argolide*; this event would be of no interest had I not heard, through local gossip, that it's on this very ship that young Lecourt is returning to his hometown; yes, Thomas Lecourt, who five years ago left his father's house to roam the world and live his life, and whom everyone called the prodigal son from that moment on. You know his father, the old man with the stern face who recently underwent an operation on his liver; you also know that he lives not far from here in a villa hidden among eucalyptus trees; from our balcony can be seen the villa's park. This old man, long a widower, hardly ever leaves the house; he attributes a great importance to butter and has devoted long hours to the study of its preparation throughout the ages; his friends sometimes jokingly call him the 'butterologist' but he does not get angry, in fact he seldom gets angry and his smile under his white mustache is always sad; often he stares into space in front of him, though there are moments when a flash of anger passes through his eyes; his features contract, his hands clutch the arms of the chair and then in a voice trembling with anger, hate, and pain he says these three words: 'Oh! the scoundrel!' It's that he has happened to glance at the portrait of Clotilda, his daughter Clotilda, hunchbacked Clotilda who was left pregnant a few months after her marriage by her husband, a handsome man with a blond mustache. But to get back to the subject, the Lecourt son is returning to his father's house; if we go out on the balcony now it shouldn't be long before we see him; there is nothing more moving, my dear friends, than such a homecoming, especially without the usual show of killing the fatted calf and the white-bearded old man stretching out his forgiving arms." Following Hebdomeros's invitation some of his friends went out onto the balcony, others took a position at the windows, and they all watched the white road that sloped down to the harbor; soon at the end of the road appeared a man who plodded wearily along, leaning on a long staff and carrying on his back a heavy bag and a coat rolled up and tied with string. The sky was covered with a thin layer of clouds and from time to time a small breeze blew very gently, whistling imperceptibly in the dry grass and telegraph wires; everything was quiet and still, but you felt that this would not last long, and it was Hebdomeros's friends who gave the signal; as soon as they saw him arrive, they all shouted together: "There he is, there he is!" and then louder still: "Three cheers for the one who has come back! Three cheers for the wanderer's return! Three cheers for the prodigal son!" These shouts and cheers spread from house to house and set the whole place in an uproar; soon flags appeared in the windows, men left their work to come and see what was happening, gangs of children started to march in front of the escort of soldiers, aping the military parade step and making with their mouths all sorts of unmentionable noises to imitate the roll of the drum. With shrill cries the swallows cut through the air in long black streaks. In the middle of the eucalyptus park the father's house maintained a stubborn silence behind its closed shutters, and as if in sympathy everything else gradually fell silent too. The noises died down; the wind held its breath, the curtains which had billowed out romantically in the open windows sank back again like flags when the wind drops. Men in shirtsleeves who had been playing billiards suddenly stopped playing as though they had become immensely weary, weary of their past life and of their present life and of the years that still awaited them, with their long procession of hours, sad or sunny, or simply neutral, neither sad nor sunny, just hours! Everyone became silent and thoughtful. A town crier, little interested in mystery and insensible to metaphysical complications, began to announce at the top of his voice the next steamer departure times and which ships took passengers as well as cargo. He was careful to precede each announcement with a violent roll of drums. A policeman coming out of a narrow, dark cul-de-sac put a stop to this sacrilege by seizing the crier and returning with him back into the passage, like a lion disappearing into the jungle again with the antelope it has taken by surprise as it drank at the water's edge. This was the moment that Hebdomeros appreciated most of all; then his appetite returned and he thought with pleasure of the noonday meal; he was far from being a glutton, he never recalled with excessive pleasure the joys of the table, but he was just a bit of a gourmand, in a discreet, intelligent way; he liked the taste of bread and grilled mutton fat and fresh, clear water and strong tobacco. He also liked Jews and everything to do with them; in the company of Jews he would relax and enjoy a sweet and strange torpor such as he felt on journeys, for when traveling he always had a slight impression of being in a dream; when he found himself with the children of Israel he also set off on a journey; a journey deep into the dark night of time and human history.

To celebrate the return of the prodigal son, a few days later the father gave a large reception to which Hebdomeros and his friends were invited. The garden of the villa was lit up by Venetian lanterns fixed to the trunks of the eucalyptus trees, and on the veranda, cleared for the occasion of all the plants and flowerpots, a buffet had been set up where the guests could find many healthy, appetizing things to eat, but no lavish extras. The sky in the west was still bright, for in this western country the long summer days stretch out very late and night falls very slowly. High in the sky the last rays of the setting sun tinted with a soft rose color one side of the little violet clouds that had arranged themselves like an amphitheater; but the countryside all around the town began to be invaded by darkness; the outlines of the trees grew dark and the whiteness of the houses faded gradually away; the noise of a train heading somewhere toward the north could be heard in the distance; the town hall clock soon struck nine; the first guests began to arrive. Hebdomeros arrived, too, surrounded by his friends, but contrary to what he had hoped and desired, his arrival and his presence was not particularly noticed. The guests refrained from dancing, out of respect for the moral suffering of the master of the house, suffering which the recent return of his son had undoubtedly alleviated though unfortunately not dispelled. Lecourt the elder had foreseen their thoughtfulness and had had the idea of entertaining them by setting up a small stage in the main drawing room of the villa and putting out several rows of chairs hired from the local café. On this stage amateur actors presented short comic sketches which were warmly applauded. Old Lecourt led the applause each time, sitting in the front row with his daughter, Clotilda, on his right and his son, Thomas, on his left. Everything was going beautifully: the party had an atmosphere of warmth, simplicity, and charm in spite of a few sly couples who, in a dreamy silence, moved off slowly toward the shadows of the park. You could have sworn that this evening would end as quietly as it had begun, when suddenly a most unfortunate incident occurred; it was caused by two of the actors in the third and final sketch; the scene of this one-act comedy was a schoolroom, and while the teacher was giving the lesson the pupils played all sorts of tricks on him. One in particular was more enterprising than the others; his specialty was to pin a little paper man, cut out of an exercise book, onto the teacher's jacket when he turned his back on the class to write on the blackboard. The actor playing the part of the teacher was a man of about fifty with a small gray mustache that curled up at the ends. He was an old acquaintance of the master of the house and was particularly irascible and punctilious by nature; it was said he had been a consul in the East and that he loved hunting grouse. Just as the actor playing the part of the mischievous pupil pinned the little man onto the tail of his jacket for the tenth time, he suddenly turned around, no doubt feeling that the other was overdoing things, and said in a dry tone: "Sir, you are going too far." To which the other replied, just as indignantly, "And you, Sir, are forgetting that we are actors on a stage, and that what we are representing is purely fiction. Besides, having had the honor of knowing you for quite some time, I believe that you've never been able to take a joke." Though in fact it was quite justified, this reply was the last straw and drove the ex-consul into a fury; he lost all self-control and, stepping forward, he slapped his fellow actor in the face. The spectators rushed onto the stage, and with the help of the other actors, they separated the two men; but it was only the presence of the venerable master of the house, leaning on his two children for support, which finally calmed the overexcited guests. The entertainment was abandoned. The audience moved off to the buffet, talking excitedly and emotionally about this unpleasant incident, while the ex-consul's wife, leading away her husband, who was still pale with rage, toward the eucalyptus trees in the garden, declared loud enough to be heard by all: "I'm proud to have a husband like that!"

The party was almost over; the last guests, including Hebdomeros, were paying their respects to the master of the house and his children before leaving the villa, whose grounds were already hidden in darkness. Outside, the sky was an unforgettable sight: the constellations were so clearly arranged that they formed real pictures drawn in dots like the illustrations in dictionaries. Hebdomeros was delighted; he stopped and began to point them out, which was not difficult as they were so easily recognizable that even someone who knew nothing whatsoever about astronomy would have known them. You could see the Heavenly Twins, leaning against each other in a tranquil, classical pose, and the Great Bear, chubby and poignant, dragging his furry hide along through the deep, dark ether; and further away there were Pisces, the Fish, slowly revolving and always staying the same distance apart as though they were fixed to the same axis, and Orion; lonely Orion was moving away into the depths of the heavens with his club on his shoulder and his faithful Dog at his heels. The Virgin, with her beautiful, generously proportioned body, lay on a cloud and turned her head gracefully as she looked down at the world still asleep in these last hours of the night; further over to the left was Libra, the Scales, with their pans lying horizontally, empty and motionless and held in perfect balance; there were constellations to suit all tastes and to satisfy the strangest of whims. Night-owl instincts were aroused in everyone. Nobody felt like going home now. Hebdomeros, who felt every emotion more intensely than other people and was always ready to give way to enthusiasm, at the expense of self-control, immediately suggested going to a little café which stayed open until morning to cater to the workmen and engineers who worked all night repairing the railroad, and who came there to take a break and have a snack.

Down in the harbor fishing boats were weighing anchor; the noise of traffic came from the main road and lights were going on in the windows of the houses; you could feel that daylight was not far away; all around, things were gradually coming to life again. Fresh breezes from the sea passed into the air like a silent call; in the east the sky grew clear. "Insomnia," Hebdomeros suddenly said to himself, and a cold shiver ran down his spine for he knew what that meant … , he knew them only too well, those mornings followed sleepless nights, summer nights filled with phantoms of the great sculptures of antiquity, nights when the specters of famous temples that vanished centuries ago stand out majestically against the dark sides of mountains; he knew them well, the hot days that followed the nights filled with visions, and the relentless sun, the insistent chirping of the sacred, invisible cicadas and the fruitless search for freshness at noon by the banks of a muddy river.

"But," thought Hebdomeros, "what does the dream about a battle by the edge of the sea mean, with canoes pulled up onto the beach and trenches hastily dug in the sand, and over there behind the trenches tiny hospitals, cute, perfect little hospitals where even the zebras, yes the poor wounded zebras, are cared for gently and skillfully and emerge all bandaged up, stitched together again, patched up, mended, disinfected—in fact, as good as new! Could it be that life is nothing but an immense lie? Nothing but the shadow of a fleeting dream? Is it nothing but the echo of the mysterious blows that resound on the rocks of that mountain over there, whose opposite side has apparently never been seen, and on whose summit can be seen by day dark masses, with an irregular profile, that are probably forests and from which at night come sighs and stifled groans as though a giant were chained up there and suffering without hope under the great, shimmering star-filled sky?" Thus spoke Hebdomeros to himself, and in the meantime night had once more fallen over the metropolis. People passed by him in a regular, continuous flow, as if they were riveted to a chain in perpetual motion. They looked at him without seeing him and saw him without looking at him; their faces were all identical; now and then some separated themselves from their invisible chain and stopped before the blinding windows of the jewelers' shops. *Cameo*, *Luxus*, *Irradio*—these were the sonorous names of the now-famous diamonds that had once adorned the crowns of monarchs assassinated by moonlight in their palaces hidden deep in dark parks. Now these priceless stones threw out in all directions their iridescent darts and their miniature northern lights; standing on little cube-shaped bases covered with red velvet, they sparkled with dazzling brightness in the center of the shopwindow, as a star shines on a calm summer night in the far corner of the sky, a star that for centuries has witnessed wars, cataclysms, and plagues striking the world and destroying what man had created. Sometimes a sure, rapacious hand, like the sharp talons of an adult vulture, would emerge between the heavy drapes that formed the backdrop of this brilliantly illuminated, obscene little theater, where luxury, the hypocritical mask of lust, shamelessly flaunted its malevolent fires. And then rebellions broke out like storms in burning summer skies. Fierce, determined men, led by a man like a colossus with the beard of an ancient god, snatched huge wooden beams from building sites and hurled them like catapult missiles at the armor-clad doors of the hotels. Some had prudently fled; others had fallen at the first exchange of blows, and they were precisely those who had refused to believe there was a rebellion and had maintained that the rumors which circulated were entirely unfounded; the rumors had been started, they said, by money-grabbing bankers trying to provoke a slump in the stock exchange so that they could speculate on the rise that would follow when it was seen to be a false alarm. It was these same people who always ended their optimistic arguments with phrases like: *Our nation has too much common sense to...* etc., etc....

It was certainly not the time to think of work. Hebdomeros had long since accepted this and had said so to his friends, so they were not surprised to see him, usually so active, spend whole days sitting in an armchair, with his feet on a stool, smoking a pipe and dreamily contemplating the ornamental molding on the ceiling. There was no news from the palace, that luxurious mansion in an unimaginable disorder, guarded by two enormous watchdogs at its main gate that with people they knew were as gentle as lambs, but as soon as they sighted a stranger the hair bristled on their backs and they barked ferociously, foaming at the mouth. Once you had gone up the majestic staircase leading from the grounds to the interior of the palace and entered a confusing maze of corridors, vestibules, halls, antechambers, and reception rooms, with folding screens placed before heavy doors; and when in bygone days footmen still carried halberds and ran behind the carriages with smoking torches in their hands, the bodies of noblemen often lay with their fists clenched and their beards in the air, noblemen treacherously stabbed to death; at this point you were obliged to take a guide, so you asked a tail-coated steward, who walked in front of you to show you the way. You felt a lightness coming over you then, your soul felt weightless like the souls of the dead, you were like Alcestis following Hercules to join her husband, and thus surrounded by an atmosphere of mythology you came to the door of the bachelor's bedroom. The unmade bed and the walls covered with photographs signed with dedications spoke of many tragedies and regrets; *he*, for he was the man Hebdomeros was seeking, was lying on the bed with his legs apart; he was wearing a short shirt that hardly reached his groin and left his sexual organ exposed with its swollen veins; the bandages and boxes of cotton balls that had been used to tend his swollen knee were scattered on top of small oriental tables inlaid with mother-of-pearl and which made one think of the somber Orient and of those hapless victims sewn into sacks and thrown at the deepest hour of the night into the dark waters of the bay. Then Hebdomeros thought of *deliverance*, of flying machines and invincible phalanxes of white warriors with helmets of gold, who would crush the enemy under their avenging heels and, in a world finally restored to peace, would regenerate humanity in the shadow of their sky-blue standards.

The masks which hid people's faces fell one after the other. Hebdomeros was quickly reassured; he had imagined their hidden faces to be highly alarming, but they had peaceful expressions that inspired the greatest confidence. A sensual cowardliness, a fierce desire for peace and bourgeois living came over everyone and then, slowly, without jostling, they moved into the solid, banal decor of those rooms whose gilt-framed mirrors were covered with thin purple muslin so that the flies shouldn't soil them. The people began to converse on the divans and sofas and from one armchair and another. Hebdomeros told, for perhaps the hundredth time, how he had met that friend who later accompanied him on all his journeys and of his passionate love, as a child, for big trees, especially the oak and the plane tree. Then, addressing a young lady, he described how he had felt the first time he had gone to the dentist to have a tooth out. "Yes, madam," he said, feeling rather excited, as he always did in the presence of this blonde woman with the strong legs and cat's eyes, "yes, madam, I was sitting in the waiting room; my feet were cold and my stomach was queasy. To take my mind off things, I concentrated on an oleograph on the wall in front of me depicting Red Indians on horseback chasing a herd of wild buffalo across a bush-covered plain. Suddenly I heard the muffled sound of an upholstered door being opened behind the waiting room door, which opened in its turn, and there stood an athletic-looking man with owl-like bespectacled eyes, wearing a long white smock. I got up quickly and said in an assured voice: 'Good morning, doctor.' He bowed silently and waved me into his consulting room. Then I walked forward slowly, holding my head up and looking straight in front of me; my mind was a complete blank..." Hebdomeros ended his story with these solemn words:

"At that moment I may have experienced the sublime ecstasy known to heroes, as well as the vile, base prostration known to the slave, his face to the ground." But the lady, whom he expected to impress by this speech, was looking at him indulgently, with a surprised, ironic expression, smiling at him as though he had just sung a song in a language she did not understand.

"And moreover," said a solidly built, red-faced man in his fifties, "it's having presence of mind that often saves a man's life. The prince who was attacked by eight outlaws in the pay of the antimonarchists would certainly have died, had he not thought of picking up one of the wrought-iron garden tables and using it as shield. I should add that he had first taken the precaution of putting out the lights, which prevented the assassins from aiming straight and made it easier for him to escape. The next day the people, wild with joy, cheered him in the square in front of the church, while fireworks went off, bells rang merrily, and pretty village girls in regional costume, their faces flushed with excitement, brought him presents of all kinds in baskets lined with costly embroidery. At that very moment he came face-to-face with a pale woman whose expression was bitter; she was that unique, wonderful woman who for ten long years had the strength and determination to hide her shame and despair from the world, even from her mother and father; he somehow found the courage to say in a voice cracking with emotion: 'God forgive me, madam, no, I am not the king.'"

The conversations would have gone on indefinitely, were it not that dusk was slowly gathering in the drawing room. Under the effect of the darkness, which began to make felt its weight, the discussions diminished in intensity, each person seemed to withdraw into himself and to think about his own problems as well as about the still-unresolved mysteries that hover over the life of men, as seagulls hover over the storm-tossed sea. In an attempt to dispel the *Stimmung* created by the fall of dusk, Hebdomeros proposed lighting the lamps but seeing that no one moved he got up to light them himself. He had barely left his chair when he felt someone grabbing his forearm; he turned and recognized in the shadows a man wearing a black tie who had an elongated chin and smooth, bony face; the aspect of his physique had struck him as being particularly unpleasant when he had first entered the drawing room. "No, sir," said the man, politely but firmly, "wait; don't light the lamps yet. Let's stay in this semidarkness while it lasts. Notice how people and objects all look more mysterious in this dim light. It's the phantoms of people and things that we see, phantoms which, once light arrives, disappear into their unknown kingdom. The outlines of things lose their hardness as they did in the periods when the art of painting reached its highest point of perfection. I am talking to you as an artist, sir, and I can assure you that I have often stayed in my studio, without lighting the lamps, as night began to fall over the town. At such times I lose myself in strange reveries as I watch my paintings sinking into a fog ever thicker and darker, as though they were entering another world, another sphere where I could never reach them. I love the hour of twilight, and even when night has fallen I leave my lamps unlit, then to go out I have to grope like a blind man for my stick and hat, bumping into chairs and easels as I make my way to the door and go down into the street. Yes, I love this hour, I have always loved it. I know that some people prefer bright light, the light of the sun at noon on city squares and streets, full of life and activity, or at the seaside, where the water shimmers like a pool of molten metal. Such people go to cafés and theaters at night, drawn by the light of hundreds of lamps, whereas I love the shadows of twilight; they are much more hospitable and restful, and they make me daydream—I can't help it. And that is why, dear friend,"—and he tightened his grip on Hebdomeros's forearm, which he had clung to throughout his speech—"I beg you, I plead with you once again: do not light the lamps." Hebdomeros, who had had to force himself to listen to all this, gazed thoughtfully at the speaker, who was sitting in a large, red velvet armchair, and whose strange face was now almost hidden in darkness. He reflected sadly on the stupidity and incommensurate selfishness of this man who, to satisfy his dubious romantic yearnings, was prepared to keep dozens and dozens of people in darkness, without it occurring to him that there might be among them some photomaniacs, i.e., people who passionately loved light, and perhaps some scotophobes, people who were afraid of the dark. It was simply revolting.

For the rest, Hebdomeros adapted quite well to a society free of intellectual complications but cordial and hospitable to the highest degree. Nevertheless, there was no lack of maniacs, and there were even a few lunatics. Among these was an art teacher who lent young people sums varying between eight and fifteen francs, at high interest, against a collateral of clothes or parts of clothing; the collateral he preferred was shirts and vests. He laid all the deposits neatly in drawers and closets and each one had a tag, attached to a button by a piece of string, bearing the name and address of the owner, the date of the transaction, the sum of money lent, etc.

Sometimes after lunch he took a friend by the arm and said in a mysterious tone: "At two o'clock I have to see someone on important business." But this important business consisted simply in meeting one of the people who owed him money, who had given him a shirt or a waistcoat against a loan of twelve francs, and offering to let him have the waistcoat back if he repaid the sum of five francs. Sometimes this art teacher's transactions were, morally speaking, highly dubious. Among his acquaintances there was a young man whose absentmindedness was notorious and who lost things with the greatest ease. The art teacher exploited his young friend's weakness in the following way: he showed him artificial jewelry of no value whatsoever, tiepins, rings, cuff links, bracelets, and the like. He bought this jewelry from small junk dealers in the out-of-the-way quarters of the town and often got them for a penny or two from tramps he met in the course of his nocturnal wanderings. When showing them off, he waxed lyrical over their beauty and value. If his absent-minded friend had the misfortune to show particular interest in one of these trinkets, he looked brokenhearted and, laying both hands on his friend's shoulder and looking intently into his eyes, said in a pathetic voice: "My dear fellow, this piece of jewelry would be yours if only it were not a family souvenir to which I am greatly attached. But as you like it so much, take it; I'll lend it to you for a while. I'll be only too happy to do this for you." His delighted friend took the false jewel and, of course, two days after at the latest he had lost it. Whereupon the art teacher wailed and moaned about the sentimental and material loss this meant to him and after much lamentation he finally succeeded in being refunded a sum at least twenty times what he had paid for the trinket. Those were the main reasons, the fundamental reasons, that incited Hebdomeros to quit this society. Where? How? Why? He could not answer these questions himself. Memories, people will say! *Memories!* What a deep resonant word, so evocative and full of feeling! It grips you simply to say it, or even read it. But this time it was not a question of a memory. Hebdomeros had gone out onto the balcony of his hotel room. It was only one step, one step off the carpet, which displayed all the horror of a lion hunt in Africa, from the room to the balcony, a balcony that was neither too high nor too low; Hebdomeros hated vertiginously high balconies; this one was just right. In the middle of it was a flagpole without a flag, attached by cables to the scrollwork of the wrought-iron balustrade. In the past this balcony had been used by demagogues, rousing the crowds to hysteria with their impassioned, ringing words, and making thousands of mouths, gaping in crimson, sweating faces, scream their faith in the meridian heat or in the shadowy torch-lit night. Now there was nothing to be seen but a few rustic stools, standing around tables of rough-hewn wood; now and then, from the top of the centuries-old plane trees which gave shade to this peaceful spot, a dried-up leaf fell in circles onto the empty, deserted tables. Close by there was a cool, clear spring, pouring over a few earthenware jugs filled with amber-colored wine. This was more than enough to arouse the enthusiasm of Casca, the painter who hailed from the south. Addressing himself to Hebdomeros, he expressed his emotion simply but lyrically: "Now *there's* happiness for us artists," he said. "What do we need, after all, to be happy? A couple of apples on a table with salt and pepper, a ray of sunlight on the floor, a sweet, faithful woman to lighten the burden of life; and last and most important—" and here he paused for a moment to look around the circle of people listening to him—"last and most important, a clear conscience. Yes, a clear conscience, to be able, rather to have the right, in the evening when, tired from the day's work, we stretch out in bed to enjoy a well-earned rest, to have the right to say not only the famous words: *I too am a painter*, which is all very fine, but which unfortunately is not everything, but also the less famous but not less important words: *I too am an honest man*." This kind of talk always got on Hebdomeros's nerves. He had heard it before. His instinctive friendliness, reinforced by his high intelligence and his extremely refined upbringing, often led him to make the best of things and to listen politely to the ravings of these maniacs, whose incommensurable logic was equaled only by their madness, sometimes obvious, but sometimes also so difficult to detect that no one noticed it, except for psychiatrists of genius who had specialized in such cases—and even then ...!

For some time Hebdomeros avoided this society and one day leaving a restaurant fairly late at night with his friends he stopped on the edge of the pavement and exclaimed: "Why do we have all these revolutions? Masses rising up like mountains shaken by earthquakes? Why these *credos* murmured in the mournful obstinate whisper of a grim purpose in life, uncompromising, seeing everything in straight lines, longing for a deleterious purity, needled by the wish for something better, something perfect; and all this in a desert country where every seed rots or dies fruitless?" Hebdomeros asked these questions of himself rather than his friends and never succeeded in finding an answer. He would have liked to interrogate those muscular ascetics who, momentarily resting from their brutal exercises, took on styled and noble poses as though they wished to hide, both to their brother fighters and to the profane onlookers, the weariness that tortured their leaden limbs. But most of the time these muscular ascetics did not reply. They looked at Hebdomeros with contemptuous irony and, outside the stadium, nudged each other and snickered when they met him. This attitude, malicious, taciturn, and irritating, was quite understandable. Their profession was difficult, and despite the undeniable beauty of the performances they gave the citizens, one could hardly say that they rolled in riches. On Sundays, when they organized sham fights in front of the prefect and his wife, they began training at five o'clock in the morning and during the winter months by lamplight. More than once the prefect's wife had begged her husband to spare these athletes their early morning rehearsals and to limit themselves to the *tableaux vivants*, which showed the death of Patroclus, fights between the Greeks and Trojans, and other episodes drawn from the poems of Homer. But these sweet continuous requests were in vain. Sometimes extraordinarily pathetic scenes took place. The prefect worked in a cool room looking out onto a garden. The windows were open and the blinds lowered. Hebdomeros loved those blinds; sometimes, finding himself at the prefect's house, he would spend whole half hours looking at them and lose himself in dreams before them, seeing there a peaceful countryside full of tranquil poetry; lakes surrounded by hills on which castles and villas raised their harmless towers and pointed roofs; ducks floating by the water's edge; fishermen drying their nets in the sun, and old folk concluding their life tranquilly in perfect conjugal harmony, winding their way slowly toward the church whose bell tower dominated the village houses like a hen surrounded by her chicks. When the prefect's wife appeared Hebdomeros withdrew discreetly into the small dining room nearby that always smelled strongly of melon. The prefect's wife then, with slow steps, approached her husband, who continued to work at his table without raising his head. She was very beautiful with her black headband framing a face the color of ivory; her handsome matronly form was revealed rather than hidden by her dress; coming close to the prefect she slipped to the floor beside his chair, and, with her arms on the knees of her husband, kneeling before him on the hard parquet, her beseeching face turned toward this taciturn, intransigent man, she gazed at him, her cheeks wet with tears. There was a scent of furniture wax and wine spirits in the air; some of the furniture was covered up, the parquet, zealously polished, had an extremely slippery surface. She begged him to spare the athletes their fatigue and strain. All, alas, in vain! The evening of the appointed day, the *tableaux vivants* took place. Up to the last moment one had hoped for an "act of God"; something that would have prevented the performance from taking place: an earthquake, a revolution, the passage of a comet, a tidal wave; but, as always in these circumstances, nothing happened; everything took place in calm and perfect order. Hebdomeros mixed with the crowds that filled the restaurants; he still hoped for the "unexpected"; he questioned the people around him, read the papers, lent an attentive ear to the conversation of his neighbors at the next table. Nothing; not a cloud on the horizon; dead calm everywhere: in heaven and on earth. So he had to bow before the inevitable. That evening, surrounded by friends, he attended the performance and *understood everything*. The riddle of this ineffable group of warriors, of pugilists, difficult to describe and forming in a corner of the drawing room a block, multicolored and immobile in its gestures of attack and defense, was deep down understood by himself alone; he realized this at once when he saw the facial expressions of the other spectators. The fact of being the only person present to comprehend a thing so rare and profound worried him. He felt a sudden fear, the fear of solitude, the desolation of loneliness, and he spoke to his friends of his fears. But imagine his astonishment when these latter, instead of commiserating or pessimistically commenting on the intellectual capacities of their contemporaries, crowded around him and, grasping his arms and his hands, cried all together: "But enjoy yourself, sir, that's the important thing!"

Hebdomeros went home that evening with a heavy heart. Those principles that he cherished and wanted carved in stone like the laws of Moses were no longer worthy in his eyes. Far distant, beyond the accumulated habits and regulations, submissive as sheep, as sheep herded in their pens waiting the fatal hour of the slaughterhouse, he saw two symbolic figures, Pity and Work, growing smaller and smaller as they withdrew, hand in hand, toward the distant low horizon. But, Great God!

How confused it all was. Charming ribbons, flames without heat darting like greedy tongues, disturbing bubbles, lines drawn with a mastery even the memory of which he had thought long lost, soft waves, persistent and unvarying, rose and rose incessantly toward the ceiling of his room. It all took off in spirals, in regular zigzags, or straight and slow, or perfectly perpendicular like the lances of disciplined troops. To create, to search, to remold, to live again, to break those stupid laws that human ignorance had created across the centuries, without at the same time falling into worse errors, and to avoid those impressions, the strongest Hebdomeros had ever known, that at times exceeded his intellectual powers. There was in his mind then a strange company, like a crowd in the streets; so many powerful possibilities that it made him bear a grudge with reality. And what man following a new idea had not, at least once in his life, abandoned the chase to follow yet another new idea encountered along the road and judged even more seductive than the first . . . Judging from previous experiences, Hebdomeros thought that the spiritual fever which laid him low at the moment would last no longer than the preceding fevers. And as he supposed that all would *come back to him again* he allowed his thoughts to linger that evening beyond the prescribed limits.

But he knew too well, alas, whence came all these difficulties and intestinal conflicts. The spades and the scythes covered with rust lay in the farmyards near the overturned ploughs, ploughshares pointing to the sky; the lazy ruffians yawned and stretched themselves enough to dislocate their bones, having emptied the last pitcher of wine. *By work thou shalt be saved and thou shalt save them*; the lictors, the deputies bearing on their athletic chests the insignia of absolute authority, had written this in chalk on the door of his house one night when all slept and a heavy silence weighed on the land because the ceiling was very low and even the insects, that usually made a thousand small noises among the grasses and the plants, that night were still. Your life will be your life! Go and take action. May a solemn and sustained music accompany you in your difficult task with another song, a song of infinite sweetness, that neither gods nor men can ever begrudge you. After all, all that can only strengthen your structure and increase your prodigious gifts, which develop each year more and more and are fruitful like a fecund tree, thus justifying your existence and sanctifying your journey on this earth among the crowd of your contemporaries. Are we not all brothers, and sisters, and friends, and even more? Are we not all travelers, sailing on the same ship past the shores strung along our way that, slowly but surely, change their dry, rocky, and inhospitable look to a sweeter, more smiling one? And these changes, these new joys, these stabilizations give already to the living man on the earth a foretaste of the joys of heaven, and Hebdomeros had foreseen them as he had foreseen the war and the ensuing peace, and other calamities and joys of mad, anxious humanity.

Try to be happy and good! It was with these words that Hebdomeros usually greeted farewell to his servants, who left him sulkily after having stolen from him and sucked him dry. But at present he also felt more at ease; he still dreamed, yes; he followed his foolish fancies, but in a more normal fashion, as an amateur, free from frenzy, from tears, from ridiculous and mock-heroic decisions. He had *achieved* something. It was certainly not a cyclopean work, one of those sustained and powerful tasks that force the respect of the most skeptical and oblige future generations to bow before *The Complete Works* ... But at least there was something. He had not completely *wasted his day*; the corners of the room were clean now, the empty cans were placed neatly in cupboards with a consoling symmetry; the shapes were progressing, several canvases were sketched out and some nearly finished. But now the hour of rest had sounded; Hebdomeros felt a gentle slumber invade his limbs; he found it difficult to raise his eyelids; sleep claimed him more and more; so he stretched out his legs in the fresh clean sheets, yawned in executing the notes of a descending scale, and turning onto his left side he slept the sleep of the just.

To sleep the sleep of the just! What man really has the right to believe himself *just*? "Art sanctifies all," so men sometimes believe. But basically all that is only an escape, speeches and pleas to appease the conscience and avoid the annoyance of remorse and the scrutiny of those who rightly or wrongly stand before you as judges if not executors. And then, thought Hebdomeros, one flees to the next exile. They were not unknown to him, those men with the heroic attitudes as long as peace and tranquility reigned around them, but who vanished before the threat of danger and afterward formed colonies, true societies of mutual aid where they recognized one another by imperceptible signs to which they alone possessed the key. "Since you are here, you are therefore my brother and my accomplice; *we are in the same situation*; we can walk arm in arm under the palm trees that border this uneventful sea, past these expensive but charming luxury hotels, armored in a formidable fashion against a thousand dangers that the ordinary man, the father of a family, the bearded and spectacled worker, the hairy man busily running about the railway platform with a small valise in his hand, his shoes dusty, his forehead sweaty, despised by all the pretty women powdering their noses at the windows of the Pullman cars, cannot in the least imagine." So spoke those men whom Hebdomeros had long known but with whom he could never be on cordial terms because he did not respect them. There was, finally, down there the complete relaxation. At last! At last alone! The mountain, that high enormous thing, swollen, black as a gigantic amphibious animal cast upon the beach, hid the discouraging sight of law-bound cities. And yet all was not rose-colored in these lands, as Hebdomeros well knew, and he was always on his guard; the beautiful scenery, those aspects of nature that seemed to have been created with joy by a charming and well-meaning God, had never inspired in him an unconditional confidence. The terrain was so irregular that one had to be an acrobatic genius to cross the mountains; impressive rocks rose almost perpendicularly from a dark deep sea. Sometimes one followed the bed of a dried-up river strewn with enormous blocks of stone and on the shore passages had to be opened with dynamite. Water was lacking; one followed the line of the coast using the beaches to pass around the rocks, as Hebdomeros was in the habit of doing, but at the risk of being caught by the incoming tide, which had happened to him several times and had placed him in a precarious position. But he always consoled himself with his labors, which, for that matter, he could easily have avoided, by speculating on the various philosophical problems that had particularly haunted him during this late summer. "Taking into consideration the increasing materialistic and pragmatic orientation of our civilization," he said to his friends, as they walked along in regular, rhythmical steps, "it is not paradoxical to visualize, as of now, a social state where the man who lives only for the pleasures of the mind will no longer have the right to claim a place in the sun. The writer, the thinker, the dreamer, the poet, the metaphysician, the observer, the fortune teller, the prophet, the soothsayer, the scrutinizer, the reasoner, the questioner of enigmas, the appraiser, the seer, the seeker of new songs, the selector of paintings of the very first class, etc., will all become anachronous, destined to disappear from the face of the earth like the ichthyosaur and the mammoth. Yes, you will tell me now that at the same time there are those who practice a philosophy according to a high ideal whose mark on the souls and minds of men can never be effaced. Thus they theorize on words and phrases that strike the mind with their monumental ring such as: *the weakness of the strong, Vocation and Renown*, or *the voice which grew silent*, and whatever else, but, basically, all that is pure nonsense, and you, my dear friends, know it as well as I. One needs the unashamed naivete of these optimistic and indulgent men to take them seriously and discuss such rubbish without bursting with laughter; and I'll go even further, I'll say that in all this, and not only in this, one can sense, without being much of a psychologist, the baseness of their aims, since in their precocious and clear positivism they no longer have the amazement of newcomers faced with the sentiments and spectacles that so deeply troubled their elders. Doubtless it is necessary for humanity to cross this dark tunnel in order to find on the other side, there where the coolness of watered gardens rises up from deep valleys, the light of this eternal idealism that is as necessary, I will even say as indispensable, to human souls as air is to the lungs. And our worth as thinking and acting beings, I say this to you, dear friends, because you are still the only ones who, up to now, have understood me; our worth is not to be found, to the same degree, in those creators of whom I am thinking. And you know who they are; even, and perhaps especially, when they give to their expressions an accent of love or the appeal of fantasy. In the first case, which, judging by the majority of opinions is the one that counts most, they present a minute portion of our humanity, the contents of a boat, even one as small as a punt, sailing between the banks of a narrow river. But you know as well as I that human beings cannot without great difficulty shake off the prejudices and pettiness that are for many the main causes of their misery in this sad world. The lesson of danger, alas, bears no fruit. Returned to the daylight, liberated from the dark cells where, during long years, they expiated errors for which, after all, they were only partly responsible, they repair to their dens to dry out their powder in the sun and sharpen the blades of their knives and daggers on polished stones gathered at the edges of streams.

"Infamous nourishment, given in full knowledge to eventualists and to those who, ignorant of any profession, trod a beaten path to slip behind the tall, squalid curtain raised a few inches only from the stage, and below which the audience, especially those seated in the front rows, can see the muddy shoes of the actors as they pass to and fro. The aim of these crafty people, full of ulterior ideas at the back of their minds, is plain: to wait until the curtain rises suddenly, to appear before the footlights violently bathed in light from head to toe, hoping for a thunderous applause to greet their appearance and later to be borne in triumph on the shoulders of a delirious crowd to the door of their hotels under the amused eyes of the porters and bellboys. Yes, but it is then precisely that things begin to get complicated, because they hope to be able to continue thus happily from pleasure to pleasure without ever seeing the reverse of the coin; they deceive themselves greatly. I, who am telling you this, dear friends, have seen that alarming kill-joy at work many times, that bald and muscular man, cold, even glacial in appearance, but whose ardent heart overflowed with passion. He was not the type of man to hesitate or waste time in boring and useless speech. He fired his pistols quickly with the precision of an expert marksman, and when he had emptied all his magazines and thrown terror into those places of luxury and pleasure, he quickly wiped his shot-blackened hands on a batiste handkerchief, calmly sat down at a table, and ate with a hearty appetite an order of ham and eggs."

Disgusted by all these sights, Hebdomeros started off with slow steps along a dusty road that led to the towns where municipal elections were taking place. Posters covered the walls; the contests between the candidates were displayed there in their own peculiar language. *Mister Sublato is addressing you only a few lines in answer to a long refutation of his administration which the Chiabani Committee has considered indispensable to bring to your present notice.*

*

*   *

Short of arguments against the Sublato Administration, judged irreproachable by all impartial people, the Chiabani Committee is seeking a change by means of involved and incomprehensible articles of the Quarry of the Cemetery.[2] *They wish to embroil the Sublato Administration in a quarrel which concerns only Mr. Chiabani and his employer, the contractor Lanteri Baptistin. Let these gentlemen argue it out in court if they have a difference of opinion. But, we beseech you, let us talk of other things than the personal interests of these two builders who have quite enough lawyers to defend them.*

*

* *

There followed the program with several projects:

1. *Construction of a scholastic group in the Moneghetti quarter with a day nursery and the creation of supplementary classes.*

2. *Construction of a dispensary for the visit of newly born infants and with a prophylactic service to fight venereal diseases, and the formation of a medical inspection for schoolchildren.*

3. *Repairs and cementing of roadways, installation of collective trash disposal units and new lamps, improvement of the public lighting system.*

4. *Tarring of the streets. Enlarging Montroni Square. Installation of a street fountain, ornamented with metaphysical figures, and containing a spacious shelter where*

---

2   Hebdomeros never succeeded in understanding the sense of these four
    words. (Author's note)

women, old folk, the disabled, and children can find when the traffic circulation is at a peak not only a safe refuge but also rest on comfortable and artistically sculptured benches.

5. Installation of an artificially lighted bowling alley where lovers of this proper and healthy recreation can enjoy their pastime even during the hours of darkness.

6. General repair of the town drainage system, with the financial aid of the state.

Then followed the appeals to the citizens, launched by those who wished to make for themselves a place in the sun:

My dear citizens,

Under the patronage of the Republican Committee of Entente and Communal Prosperity, the retiring administration has decided to solicit your votes for the renewal of its term.

The Chiabani party, which dares to speak of liberty, has given us a foretaste of how it interprets the word in preventing Mr. Sublato, our mayor, from expressing his thoughts at the Reunion of the Square Fountains. Mr. Sublato can redress these calumnies uttered against him.

Truth, uttered by an administrator of integrity like Mr. Sublato, frightens them.

Powerless to reply seriously to the arguments of Mr. Sublato, the followers of Mr. Chiabani are left with no other resources than disorder and brawling.

*
* *

The heat weighed like a leaden cope. Hebdomeros pulled out his handkerchief and wiped his dripping face. He had already passed with his friends the last houses, and all around them the countryside, scorched and desolate, had something of grandeur. The gray veils of the goddess Humidity, like the families of great migrating birds, had already flown far away toward the mists of the north. Long yellow-orange shawls of an infinite tenderness hung from the parapets of half-ruined bridges, whose low, wide arches strode the dried-up streams. Everything had about it a profoundly *calcined* quality. The undying ghosts of the *Great Heat*, brothers of the polar ghosts of the *Great Cold*, wandered everywhere, present and invisible. Hebdomeros's heart rejoiced at the sight; he and his friends stopped from time to time to solemnly remove their hats before the corpses of bandits, shot down by the gendarmes, who lay now with their clothes in tatters near the broken carbines in magnificent poses of weariness and sleep.

When the last ramparts of the town had disappeared over the horizon, Hebdomeros, feeling a little tired, asked his friends to follow him to a little grove. They left the road and soon found themselves in the shade of some trees that were pressed one against the other in a compact group as though to defend themselves against some invisible danger. Hebdomeros sat on a tree trunk lying on the ground and his friends did the same; but as they loved to hear him talk they begged him to tell them one of those stories, so perfectly logical in appearance and so greatly metaphysical at heart, of which he held the secret and the monopoly. Hebdomeros as usual needed no prodding; he stretched himself several times, yawned, scratched his stomach with pleasure, drank a few gulps from his drinking gourd of water mixed with red wine, carefully lit his pipe, and began as follows:

"My dear friends, you have probably noticed as much as I that special *Stimmung* (atmosphere) which is felt when, on coming out into the road at sunset at the end of a hot summer's day following an afternoon sleep (remember what I have already said many times on the subject of sleeping in the afternoon), one smells the scent of freshly watered streets. If the town is situated beside the sea the suggestive power of this smell is even doubled or tripled. It's what my father always said when he mentioned the town where he grew up. My father was an unusual man, whom the adventures of life, both real and supernatural, had made sensitive, gay, and suspicious. He was rather careful in his conversation and detested certain ready-made phrases like: *We all carry a stone in our sack*, or *Life is never as good nor as bad as they say*.

"He loved music, especially music rich with melodies, and he had a horror of beds with spring mattresses. His ideal bed was a wire mesh on very low wooden legs supporting a perfectly flat mattress. As for a pillow, he claimed he could never rest on those long cylinders sheathed in white cotton that give the sleeper such terrible nightmares, but only on a bolster laid across the head of the bed which, seen in section, formed an isosceles triangle. 'The Etruscans,' he said, 'who understood this matter of beds, always laid their statues on perfectly flat surfaces. Throughout the Mediterranean littoral, where this profoundly strange and mysterious people arose and disappeared, one can still see the imprint they left on the earth, there where they lay down for the last time to sleep in the arms of death. But do you see the Etruscans lying down to their final rest on hog-backed mountains? No, surely not. I believe that no man could be so phrenologically altered and, I even dare to say, so careless of the charm that derives from the equilibrium and the harmony of lines as to imagine such a monstrosity. That is why I affirm, profoundly convinced of affirming an irrefutable truth, that a wire mesh (surface absolutely flat) should, in the construction of a bed, take absolute precedence over one of those spring mattresses whose surface is convex in the middle, and the much vaunted softness of whose springs is only an illusion, or at least a very ephemeral virtue.' So spoke my father on the subject of beds. Another of his peculiarities was leukophobia, or fear of the color white. He was sincerely and deeply leukophobic. He had trained his servants to remove the dining-room tablecloth without lifting and shaking it like a sail or a flag but in carefully folding it on the table itself and carrying it away quickly like a filthy package.[3] This leukophobia haunted him more especially in the country when they cleared the table at twilight, after the evening meal on the flowered veranda of a modest villa

---

3 All these complications and upsetting problems were resolved later on by the use of colored tablecloths. (Author's note)

which he rented in order to pass with his family the hot months of summer far from town.

"He felt an enormous pity for dark-complexioned men with thick black eyebrows; he would have liked to decolorize their hairs and tint them ash blond, give to these men the appearance of charming pages, then enthrone them in the middle of a front-row box on opening night in the principal theater of a great Nordic capital. This wish, alas, he was never able to realize.

"The town where he had passed his childhood was the favorite subject of his memories; he spoke of it with love and tenderness, sometimes even with exaltation; while he talked, his eyes, blue and very gently, shone with an ineffable brilliance; he looked beyond the world and things, lost in a dream without end; 'I believe I can see it,' he said in a low and trembling voice, 'I believe I can see it, that town which has no equal. I seem to live again those late afternoons in summer after the day's heat. The engineers, having finished their work on the railway line under construction, returned to their furnished rooms, covered with dust and harassed with fatigue. Hidden behind thick clusters of oleanders, the town stretched gracefully along the foot of a mountain, imposing but harmonious in its contours; it offered its marble quays to the little waves of the port that came silently to caress them. The streets, watered with care and refreshed by the breeze, presented a gay and animated scene to the eyes. The trees that shaded them murmured softly. On green lawns the flowers in their flowerbeds opened their petals and perfumed the air. The houses smiled, calm and coquettish in their cleanliness. The air was balmy, the sky blue as the sea that one glimpsed shimmering at the end of long avenues. It was the hour when the academies of painting, music, and sculpture and the public library closed. These buildings were all to be found in the same quarter of the town, and here excellent professors taught courses open to the public, which were organized in small classes that permitted each pupil to gather to himself all the fruits of the lesson. The crowds leaving these establishments created a certain encumbrance for a short time, but no exclamation of impatience, no objection was ever heard. The general effect was one of complete calm and satisfaction. The cafés were also all that one could desire. They nearly all possessed a restaurant. The principal café, whose owner was my intimate friend, was called Café Zampani. It was a real masterpiece. Located on the corner of the main boulevard and the most important town square, it was, by its location, the center of the whole region. The business, industrial, and artistic personalities of the town met on its terrace and in its luxuriously decorated rooms. Its whole appearance revealed a sober, elegant, and distinguished art. The services of the Café Zampani profited from all the perfections that the most ingenious technical resources could offer. In the salons artificial ventilation assured an atmosphere constantly renewed by filtered air, hygrometrically humidified, and ozonized.

"'For gourmets, Café Zampani had in elaborating its menus made a selection of the best gastronomic specialties and a refined dish was served every day at each meal. The cellar was under the personal supervision of the proprietor; he chose and bought wines directly from the winegrowers and, for the service of his customers, he took great care to choose only the best years of the best vineyards.'

"Thus spoke my father," said Hebdomeros after a pause. Little by little, in recalling the past, Hebdomeros, that singular man whom even the most intelligent of his friends had never succeeded in defining, felt again the same feelings that had been awakened in him at the sight of those men condemned to death and then pardoned who bear in their young and bearded faces something of their former anguish and grief. Their arms folded, they were thoughtful and quiet, in spite of their evident muscular strength, which one surmised from the size of their deltoids and biceps that stood out under the sleeves of their tight jackets (they were poor and could not afford those handsome English suits, ample and elegant, which are the joy of intelligent men of good taste). Up there on the hillsides gilded by autumn, women, in white bodices with their sleeves rolled up, were squeezing with a strong hand black grapes into crystal cups.

Tired of all these terrestrial and metaphysical adventures, Hebdomeros went to bed and didn't awaken the following morning until very late. Once awake, he could not decide to get up, so he remained for several hours in his bed meditating, and finally deciding to look at his watch, which he always kept on a chair beside his bed, he found that it was five o'clock in the afternoon. This is the hour, thought Hebdomeros, that in the twelve months of the year corresponds to the month of September. Then he understood that it would have been *logical* for him to close his metaphysical cycle at the end of this very day. He loved logic and order even more than harmony; seeing that chance (or something else) had made him look at his watch just at that minute when the hands marked the hour that corresponded to the month of September, he should profit by this good luck and not complicate things unnecessarily. He knew that what awaited him was not happiness, such as generally understood by men; it had nothing to do with that cold feeling in the stomach, that sensation of uneasiness and anxiety, that impossibility of remaining quietly seated in one's chair, that need for loquacity and expansiveness, that desire to recount even to the first person who comes along the event which troubles us, that sort of abandon and incommensurable weakness, finally all those symptoms that we feel when a sudden happy event surprises us in the monotonous round of life. Hebdomeros, like everyone, had known such moments, not violent ones, not to the point of dying with joy like Ulysses's dog, or going insane like the painter Frank Sbysko, struck with madness the day he learned that he won a million in the lottery, but all the same important and significant enough.

But he felt, and his feelings seldom betrayed him, he felt that this time it was less a question of happiness than of security, it was a feeling of security that was going to envelop him, and he prepared himself to receive it with dignity, with composure, as the believer prepares to receive in himself, in the form of the Host or otherwise, the God he believes in. Hebdomeros opened the window of his room but he avoided taking in deep breaths of the outside air like a liberated prisoner or an invalid who feels better, etc.; besides he had no reason to do so, and nature, or better still the elements themselves, helped him to avoid these attitudes that were compromising for a serious man like himself. In fact, with regard to attitudes he could only half boast of being a wise guy in the metaphysical sense of the word. The outside air was, in fact, neither pure nor fresher than the air in his room; that does not at all mean that the air was bad, on the contrary, only that the air in the room where he happened to be was excellent and that the air outside resembled it perfectly, as one drop of water resembles another, its sister. Not a breeze; an absolute calm; in this part of town the houses were irregularly placed though near enough to one another; it was a half holiday and into every man had descended the hope of a half-god. There are now half-gods dressed like everyone else who walked the sidewalks and waited at the street corners for the cars to pass. If the fifth hour of the afternoon is that which comes between evening and the second half of the day, the month of September is that which comes between two seasons:

summer and autumn. That corresponds, in the case of a sick person, to the moment which precedes convalescence, and which, naturally, at the same time, marks the end of the malady, so to speak. In fact, summer is a malady, it's all fever and delirium and exhausting perspiration, an unending weariness. Autumn is convalescence, after which begins *life* (winter). "Yes," thought Hebdomeros, "that seems strange, it obliges me to argue with my fellow men at the risk of being seen as a madman and to feel afterward behind my back the mockery of *the logical ones*, those who think they possess the key to the causes and effects and the table of values of everything in this base world. And yet I am sure that it is not like that; these are only bad habits, false movements which humanity from its infancy has been used to making; they have contorted the way of truth, or hidden it, covered it with fogs and vapor, tarnished it, giving it the same color as the objects that surround it on earth so that it fades into the landscape and man, distracted, passes beside it and rubs against it without recognizing it, as the hunter passes, his gun slung over his shoulder, close to the motionless quail without seeing it because the color of its plumage matched the ground where it rests." Hebdomeros, this time at least knew by what he should abide and he thought with reason that if at other times he had feared happiness, and before its constant menace he had, as a gesture of exorcism, broken the urns, this time his fears would have been absolutely misplaced and completely unjustified; he did not like to do useless things unless it was a question of what he called the *necessary inutility*, but in this case it would no longer be a question of an inutility. His theories of life varied according to the sum of his experiences. What could he in this case conclude, if not that the secret of happiness, that inestimable secret that most philosophers exhaust themselves in seeking theoretically and that the immense majority of men strive practically to discover, consists, perhaps, in admiring nothing, in loving nothing? In that case skepticism? No, for that which his adversaries, at particularly delicate or serious moments, were disposed to believe in was only a half-truth, if that! That he was boasting there's no doubt, but isn't boasting often a necessary thing, even an indispensable one? And is it not better to boast, even at the risk of irritating one's contemporaries, than to be like the famous courtier, so used in the exercise of his profession that in the end he lost his memory? That which was certain, and which Hebdomeros proved each time he had the occasion to do so, was that he was infinitely less rigid in the application of his own rules of conduct when it was a question of his own self. After all, it would be really too eccentric to consider oneself superior to others without first being superior to oneself. In any case, and in spite of that great desire for justice which had always predominated in each of his acts, he felt no envy whatsoever of those who succeeded in playing this double game. Rather would he have been tempted to say that enemies were necessary. Without them existence threatened to become fairly dull and exasperatingly monotonous; he thought that enemies play an important role in the organization of social life and in the manifestations of human life in the same way that certain animals, more or less unpleasant, often rather repugnant, whose usefulness was not apparent at first glance, had nevertheless their proper place in the plan of creation. And then, can one coolly conceive of an existence where one has only the choice between admiring nothing, indeed entertaining no illusions, or keeping jealously to oneself both one's illusions and one's admirations? So Hebdomeros no longer pleaded extenuating circumstances, even to his contemporaries, among whom he included his nearest friends and his most fervent admirers, nor did he seek any other roundabout means of claiming the right to be praised. He hoped, on the other hand, and this since a long time, even during those periods of transition that had permitted him to open new doors on the most unexpected sights, that those who followed him would not blame him for using, with the proper discretion, in presenting what he modestly called *his Marvels*, a language that on any other occasion would have brought upon his shoulders not only the sarcasm of the crowd, which often is necessary to far-reaching minds, but also the sarcasm of the elite, that same elite to which he boasted, with every right, of belonging but which, to his great regret, he was obliged to renounce, as the prophet renounces his mother. This happened each time that a creation of a special character obliged him to isolate himself completely and place himself beyond good and evil, but especially beyond the good. The task, for that matter, was anything but easy. All that he said, all that he did, was said and done quite naturally to charm the most diverse tastes. There was something to please children, real children who are often formidable judges and also who often have the preponderant voice in the council; there was something to please amateurs and collectors of pictures and, above all, those big, bogus children, the artist. Ah, it's that the art of *seeing* and describing what one has seen, preceding as everyone knows the invention of poetry proper, had covered proud distances since the first attempts. And in spite of this there were always those (and this was one of his greatest regrets)—there were always those people who reproached him for stepping out of the frame that seemed to have been assigned to him by his very nature, astonished though they were by the tours de force achieved and by the innumerable difficulties overcome. For all these reasons he had acquired a privileged position from which his adversaries tried in vain to dislodge him. His particular qualities, and the talent that he continued unceasingly to perfect, preserved him without doubt from the vicissitudes of fashion. The system that he employed had advantages both sure and undeniable. He worked particularly fast and respected with a rigorous fidelity the *character*, and even what in general is the most difficult, the color of the original inspiration. At *origin*, not original; Hebdomeros distrusted "originality" as much as he distrusted fantasy;

"You must never gallop too hard on the back of fantasy," he said, "what is needed is *to discover*, for in discovering one renders life possible in the sense that one reconciles it with its mother, *Eternity*; in discovering one pays tribute to that minotaur that men call Time, and which they portray in the form of a great, withered old man, seated with a thoughtful air between a scythe and a clepsydra."

Once again Hebdomeros felt himself moored at the crossroads, the gentle swell of the waves lapping the blocks of the quay. Then eloquence and something like a new romantic inspiration came to him, and addressing his friends he said: "Nothing can replace this ineffable contentment resulting from twenty years of experience and constant effort, also nothing can surpass in evocative power that divine serenade where merge together our ignorance of ourselves, mysterious joy, the trembling or rather the throbbing of the heart at moonlight, while the rhythmic chords of guitars fall again and again one into the other as water falls into water. From our natures, from our weaknesses, from the measureless tensions where art, which is after all but an invention of man, had plunged us since puberty, memories, softened by the veil of years, pass in a silent flutter of wings. Fruitful source of failure and deception, to fight thine ignorance, O poet, follow the sage counsel of thy muse; she is there, leaning pensively on this broken column where the lizard glides and the ivy climbs ... O flowers of tenderness! Treasures! Laments! Infinite stanzas to the stars! Beating of wings! Morning songs of harvesters! Charming interludes! Offerings! Village festivals blessed under the blue sky! O pastorals! O falling leaves! Listen to the slow confession of the old violoncello, O heart that has never changed! Remember Eunice's kiss! Remember the farewell of the roses! Listen to the song of the nest on the flowering road! O unfinished symphony in these eternal *voglio amarti*! Songs without words softly chanted! Sad reveries! Remembrances! *Recuerdos!* O starry night! Juanita! Juanita! The water sings and sings on below the flowered cottages of Polish households. Waves of the Rhône and waves of the Rhine! Melancholy maps, sometimes gray and sometimes green but always blue there where the lakes lie and the vast oceans open! The moths of the night have burned their wings on acetylene lamps! The leaves of autumn, wet with the rain, tumbled, turning, onto the rotten wood of our villa balconies! What say your eyes? Forever or never! Open wide the gates of your gardens, friends with heavy hearts! We will help you in your work; we will study with you in a brotherly, friendly, cordial fashion all the propositions that you wish to make to us."

However, it was time to go home. Hebdomeros understood this and his heart drowned in a great sadness. Fatal transformations reflected to infinity the most foolish hopes, and hierarchical decisions were spread out triumphantly, printed in characters black and solemn against the whiteness of the paper. The generals themselves, high-ranking government officials and important dignitaries with obscene grins beneath greasy mustaches bowed in a false, protocol humility whose only aim was to save appearances, very questionable appearances, by the way, that would better have been dispensed with. Hebdomeros knew the rest. He knew them well, those interminable afternoons in the map room (garden side). Yes, after lunch one retired there to rest, so to speak, for it was hot, implacably hot since the first hours of the day. But once there, where was the repose? Yes, where had he flown, this gentle god, this younger brother of sleep? Nostalgias, nostalgias without end, hands clenched at the end of arms stretched out of windows whose tritely patterned white curtains blew slightly from the intermittent breath of a warm breeze that came from the fields, these fields that stretched out elbowing one another, all alike except for slight variations of color that counted for little in the monotone symphony of grays, gray-greens, ocher-grays, green-ochers, etc. And then why should one suddenly stop? And renounce the chances and possibilities of an enterprise, very costly, moreover, but which promised joys and repose unexpected and unforgettable, even though it was not an enterprise of *complete repose*, as Hebdomeros himself said, smiling ironically. But one gained nothing for nothing: giving, giving; at the gates of oriental cities under the crushing dome of a burning sky the dysenteric merchants gesticulate around their goods, thrown pell-mell in the hot dust, on which the flies with their thanatophoric—i.e., death-bearing—proboscises persist in the minuscule humming of their little, iridescent, fast-beating wings. "Yes," said

Hebdomeros, "commerce, trade, business, exchange, speculation, valorization, confidence, credit, profits, business is business, and then in the evening harassed and tired, palms dirtied by vile money, where is our reward? A handful of rotten dates, a mouthful of tepid water soiled by the birds of the sky, drunk from a bowl that smells of wet wood ... But the great reward this evening, 'tis thou, O Cornelia! Thou, shepherdess with the legs twined in ribbons and the hands of a mother! Thou, heavy gazelle, thou, little mother of the Gracchi! If in dark and sordid streets the furious commoners stoned thy son, O touching and naked as a little donkey without a packsaddle, he who perceived the light of thy glance will throw himself alone into the delirious crowd, the Monomachos before which everything retreats, he will bring thy son back in his arms, thy son bleeding but safe, thy son fainting but alive, so as finally to see the miracle of thy tears, pearls sliding at first slowly, then faster, down thy lovely cheeks, to fall on thy hands so pure, O Cornelia."

The setting changed again. Dusk had fallen. The sordid blind alleys whence rose the stench of fermenting ordure were now far away; no more massacres. The mother of the Gracchi had *evolved*, if one dare express oneself thus ...

... Mournful pedestrians, holding their children by the hand, having returned to their homes with that vague melancholy that follows the sensation of a joy completed, a happiness achieved. Hebdomeros opened wide his window on the spectacle of life, on the stage of the world. Arms folded on his chest, head high, like a navigator standing on the prow of his ship before the apparition of an unknown land, he waited. But he had to wait for it was still just a dream, or even a dream within a dream. At the horizon the sky was alight with the last glimmer of twilight. Smoke rose and rose continuously in straight columns ... Hebdomeros turned over on his bed ... "What time is it?" and he continued to talk to himself out loud. "How much longer? ... Soon the moon will rise and with it the wind and the stars ...; fleas devour me and enteritis twists my bowels. I have drunk my last drops of belladonna and henbane! What can I hope for now! In what shall I still believe? The gods emigrated; the playful joys which hide behind the bushes and from there beckon you to approach, which you are careful not to do for you will not have taken two paces toward them but they already will have flown far away, too far, alas! ... The assassins far from the cities, peace and justice prevailing everywhere. And thou whom I glimpse before my afternoon sleep; thou, visible to myself alone, thou whose glance speaks to me of immortality!"

... Distrustful, as always, he approached carefully, one hand in his trousers pocket and the other free, ready to parry the blow. Squads of heavily armed soldiers passed beside him with something obstinate and taciturn in their looks. Rockets rose in the sky, but silently, all sound was stilled. All that is hard in the world: stones of the earth, bones of men and animals, seemed to have disappeared forever; a great wave, heavy and irresistible, of an infinite tenderness, had submerged everything and, in the middle of this new Ocean, Hebdomeros's ship floated immobile, all sails still. But then, slowly, in a puzzling manner, a new and strange confidence began to be reborn in his soul. At first he was frightened; he even trembled as the sickly old man in his armchair trembles, alone in the empty manor during a winter's night, when he sees the handle of the door turn slowly, moved from outside by a mysterious hand. Then suddenly, swept by an irresistible blast of air, fear, anguish, doubt, nostalgia, discontent, the alarms, the despairs, the fatigues, the incertitude, the cowardice, the weakness, the disgust, the mistrust, the hate, the anger, all, all disappeared in a great tornado, there behind the little half-ruined brick walls around which the brambles and nettles were clinging like a tenacious malady. Waves whose murky depths were wholly embroidered on the surface with surging foam and great masses of wild mares, hooves hard as steel, disappeared in an unbridled gallop, in an avalanche of rumps rubbing together, colliding, pushing toward infinity ...

And once more it was the desert and the night. Once again all slept in stillness and in silence. Suddenly Hebdomeros saw that this woman had the eyes of his father; and he *understood*. She spoke of immortality in the great starless night.

... "O Hebdomeros," she said, "I am Immortality. Nouns have their gender, or rather their sex, as you once said with much finesse, and the verbs, alas, decline. Have you ever thought of my death? Have you ever thought of the death of my death? Have you *thought of my life*? One day, O brother ..."

But she spoke no further. Seated on the trunk of a broken column, she placed a hand gently on his shoulder, and with the other she clasped the right hand of the hero. Hebdomeros, his elbow on the ruin and his chin in his hand, pondered no longer ... His thoughts, in the pure breath of that voice that he had just heard, yielded slowly and abandoned him altogether, surrendering to the caressing waves of unforgettable words they floated toward strange and unknown shores. They floated in the warmth of the setting sun, smiling in its descent toward the cerulean skies ...

Meanwhile, between the sky and the vast stretch of the seas, green islands, marvelous islands, passed slowly, as pass the ships of a squadron before the vice admiral, while a long sacred procession of heavenly birds, of an immaculate whiteness, flew by singing.

Paris, October 1929

The Italian painter GIORGIO DE CHIRICO (1888–1978) is best known for developing the style of metaphysical painting, which greatly influenced surrealism. Born in Greece, de Chirico studied in Athens and Munich, where he was inspired by the writings of Schopenhauer and Nietzsche and the work of Arnold Böcklin and Max Klinger. After a year in Florence, he moved to Paris in 1911 and began exhibiting his enigmatic paintings of deserted piazzas featuring Roman arcades and classical statues that cast long, illogical shadows. While serving in the Italian army during World War I, he integrated objects and depictions of canvases on easels from disorienting perspectives into his mysterious interiors and landscapes. After 1919, upon settling in Rome, he embraced the style and techniques of the Italian masters and executed more academic compositions, though by 1925 he was again living in Paris and had returned to metaphysical themes. He continued to paint until the end of his life, living between Italy and France, and at eighty years old he entered his neometaphysical period, reinterpreting the classical subjects from his early, disquieting work in serene atmospheres and bright colors.

FABIO BENZI is an expert on Giorgio de Chirico, futurism, and European avant-garde movements. He is full professor of the history of contemporary art at the University of Chieti-Pescara and a member of the board of the Fondazione Giorgio e Isa de Chirico. He has written seminal publications on twentieth-century Italian art and has curated exhibitions worldwide.

"Ekphrasis" is traditionally defined as the literary representation of a work of visual art. One of the oldest forms of writing, it originated in ancient Greece, where it referred to the practice and skill of presenting artworks through vivid, highly detailed accounts. Today, "ekphrasis" is more openly interpreted as one art form, whether it be writing, visual art, music, or film, that is used to describe another art form, in order to bring to an audience the experiential and visceral impact of the subject.

The *ekphrasis* series from David Zwirner Books is dedicated to publishing rare, out-of-print, and newly commissioned texts as accessible paperback volumes. It is part of David Zwirner Books's ongoing effort to publish new and surprising pieces of writing on visual culture.

OTHER TITLES IN THE *EKPHRASIS* SERIES

On Contemporary Art
César Aira

Something Close to Music
John Ashbery

The Salon of 1846
Charles Baudelaire

My Friend Van Gogh
Émile Bernard

Strange Impressions
Romaine Brooks

A Balthus Notebook
Guy Davenport

That Still Moment
Edwin Denby

Ramblings of a Wannabe Painter
Paul Gauguin

Thrust: A Spasmodic Pictorial History of the Codpiece in Art
Michael Glover

Visions and Ecstasies
H.D.

Mad about Painting
Katsushika Hokusai

Blue
Derek Jarman

Kandinsky: Incarnating Beauty
Alexandre Kojève

Pissing Figures 1280–2014
Jean-Claude Lebensztejn

The Psychology of an Art Writer
Vernon Lee

Degas and His Model
Alice Michel

28 Paradises
Patrick Modiano and
Dominique Zehrfuss

Any Day Now: Toward a Black Aesthetic
Larry Neal

Summoning Pearl Harbor
Alexander Nemerov

Chardin and Rembrandt
Marcel Proust

Letters to a Young Painter
Rainer Maria Rilke

The Cathedral Is Dying
Auguste Rodin

Giotto and His Works in Padua
John Ruskin

Duchamp's Last Day
Donald Shambroom

Dix Portraits
Gertrude Stein

Photography and Belief
David Levi Strauss

Souvenirs
Élisabeth Louise Vigée Le Brun

The Critic as Artist
Oscar Wilde

Oh, to Be a Painter!
Virginia Woolf

Two Cities
Cynthia Zarin

Hebdomeros
A novel by Giorgio de Chirico

Published by
David Zwirner Books
520 West 20th Street, 2nd Floor
New York, New York 10011
+ 1 212 727 2070
davidzwirnerbooks.com

Editor: Elizabeth Gordon
Proofreader: Anna Drozda
Project intern: Maia Cornish-Keefe

Design: Michael Dyer / Remake
Production manager: Luke Chase
Color separations: VeronaLibri,
Verona
Printing: VeronaLibri, Verona

Typeface: Arnhem
Paper: Holmen Book Cream, 80 gsm

Publication © 2025
David Zwirner Books

Hebdomeros © 2025
Fondazione Giorgio e Isa de Chirico,
Rome

Introduction © 2025
Fabio Benzi

The introduction was first
published in Italian in *Ebdòmero*
by La nave di Teseo, Milan, in 2019.
Translated from the Italian by
Antony Shugaar and edited for this
volume.

"Epistle to Giorgio de Chirico"
by Silvina Ocampo © 2025 Heirs of
Silvina Ocampo

The English translation of
Hebdomeros, from the original
French edition published in 1929,
remains unattributed. The present
translation has been slightly revised
by Mary Katherine Robinson in
collaboration with the Fondazione
Giorgio e Isa de Chirico to better
reflect the original text.

p. 5: Musée d'Art Moderne de Paris.
Image © 2025 Artists Rights Society
(ARS), New York/SIAE, Rome

Distributed in the United States
and Canada by
Simon & Schuster, Inc.
1230 Avenue of the Americas
New York, New York 10020
simonandschuster.com

Distributed outside the
United States and Canada by
Thames & Hudson, Ltd.
181A High Holborn
London WC1V 7QX
thamesandhudson.com

ISBN 978-1-64423-163-0

Library of Congress
Control Number: 2024949465

Printed in Italy

David Zwirner Books

ekphrasis